Anonymous

That Little Frenchman

A tale. Vol. 2

Anonymous

That Little Frenchman
A tale. Vol. 2

ISBN/EAN: 9783337146672

Printed in Europe, USA, Canada, Australia, Japan

Cover: Foto ©Andreas Hilbeck / pixelio.de

More available books at **www.hansebooks.com**

"THAT LITTLE FRENCHMAN."

A Tale.

BY THE AUTHOR OF "SHIP AHOY!"

VOL. II.

LONDON:

TINSLEY BROTHERS, 8, CATHERINE STREET,
STRAND.

1874.

LONDON ;
SWEETING AND CO., PRINTERS,
80, GRAY'S INN ROAD.

"THAT LITTLE FRENCHMAN."

CHAPTER I.

PATRIOTISM.

EMAIRE did not speak, but sat thinking of the quantity of the powder contained in the bottle. Suppose a spark should reach it from a cigarette? Suppose D'Aulnay should, in his excitement, throw down more, and it should communicate with the bottle! Or suppose he should let the bottle slip from his fingers, what would be

the result?   There could be no doubt of
that: the roof, the greater part of the house,
and of those right and left, blown to dust, and
its occupants hurled hundreds of yards in fragments.   He did not move; but the tiny dew
which glistened upon his forehead grew into
beads, and the beads ran one into the other;
and then, always growing, began to trickle
slowly down his face.

"And you, Lemaire—what do you think?"

"It is wonderful," he said, hoarsely.

"Would you like to see?"

Lemaire took the bottle held out to him,
and longed to hurl it through the window, far
away from where they stood; but he restrained
himself, and gently handed it back.

"Ah," said D'Aulnay, laughing, "you may
well use care.   My faith, it is strong.   Why,
if I were to shake it up too hard, it would
explode.   Shall I try?" he said, with a fiendish
grin.

It was evidently said to test the courage of

Lamaire; but he neither moved nor answered, leaving it to Hippolyte—who, however, was perfectly calm and unmoved as he responded—

"No, my friend; our beautiful France cannot spare three such children as we. Let us keep the glorious powder to scatter amongst her foes."

"Good," said D'Aulnay; and he carefully closed the bottle, and replaced it on his shelf.

"Ah," he said, as he pointed at the innocent-looking row of glasses, "there would not be much left of this street if one of those were to explode."

"Nor its people," said Lamaire, huskily.

By way of answer, D'Aulnay gave his shoulders a shrug which took them nearly to his ears.

"But the shells—how go the shells?" said Hippolyte. "I have not seen since yesterday."

Lemaire rose now, stifling a sigh of relief, and striving hard to conceal the ghastly look which he felt sure was upon his face in an aspect of interest in that which he was to see. But D'Aulnay evidently saw it, and smiled to himself as he led the way to his bench.

"See," he said, taking up a file, "this is how I work for the good cause."

The next moment he was rasping off tiny fragments of iron from the cup-like piece upon which he was engaged.

"There," he said, laying down his file, and turning the screw of the vice so as to loosen the iron—"there, is not that smooth, and perfect, and admirable? The iron is hard—very hard and brittle. It will hardly yield to the tools when I turn it. But what will you? It must not be rough, or it would not shatter when the powder shall explode."

He handed the cup—which was a perfect half-sphere of about three-eighths of an inch in thickness—from one to the other; and then, taking up another finished half from the bench, he fitted them together to show his visitors how they formed an iron ball about the same in size as the leather sphere used for cricket, which it was not much unlike in the way it joined, saving that the metal looked new and bright.

"It is beautiful—what pains we take for these people!—is it not?" said D'Aulnay. "What a magnificent shell this will be! I shall fill it with a mixture of my powder, and then bind the joint with an iron ring, closing it safely, so that it must break elsewhere—when the explosion follows. I shall make twenty-four of these for the dear friends who keep us here—twenty-four; although the labour is great, and the cost of the powder is frightful. But it is only an investment—eh, Lalande? We shall have it back from the brigands, with an interest on our expenditure that shall frighten them."

"'Tis so," said Monsieur Hippolyte. "We shall not fail this time, mark me—we shall not fail. It was a cursed folly, that last time. Our friends were too eager, and spoiled all."

"That poor lad Pierre is dead. Did you know?" said Lemaire.

"My faith!—my poor nephew!" said D'Aulnay. "No."

"Yes, in trying to escape from prison with Rivière."

"Ah, yes—the poor fellow who was taken."

"Yes. Pierre was shot," said Lemaire.

"He shall be avenged. Many deaths shall pay for his, poor lad. But are you sure?"

"Certain," said Lemaire. "I have it on good authority; and besides, it is here, in the provincial paper."

He handed the sheet which he took from his pocket; and, after reading it, D'Aulnay turned aside, evidently much moved.

"Poor boy!—poor boy!" he muttered again and again. "This should not have been. Only another month, my brothers, and we would have gone over and set him free, with many more. But he shall be avenged."

Monsieur Hippolyte set his teeth, grinned savagely, and went about the room gesticulating.

"But the other—Rivière—what became of him?" said D'Aulnay, suddenly turning upon Lemaire.

"Escaped."

"Good. He deserved to escape. Poor fellow, he was innocent. It was an ill fate which led to his seizure."

"Some villain must have denounced him for a grudge," said Hippolyte.

Lemaire sat unmoved till the other had finished, and then he said—

"They escaped together. Pierre was shot, and Rivière got away; but, like a fool, must go straight to Paris."

"Where he was taken?"

Lemaire nodded.

"Poor fool! poor fool!" ejaculated Monsieur Hippolyte. "It is so: these men are like the moths—they fly round and round the candle until their wings are singed."

Monsieur Hippolyte made the remark in all good faith, not then able to see any resemblance

to his metaphor in the acts of himself and his
confrères; and he kept on walking up and down
the room, while D'Aulnay bit at his moustache,
and fitted together the shell he was making,
rubbing the edges together; and at times,
as he held a half-sphere in each hand, tap-
ping them together cymbal-fashion. Then he
fitted them closely, took up a piece of tape,
and bound it round and round, ending by
tying it securely, and holding the iron ball in
his hand.

"Perdition to all our enemies!" he said.
"France shall be cleared of the canaille who
hold her by the throat and trample upon her,
poor fair mother! Ah, my brothers, the time is
nearly here, and this cursed land of fog shall
know us no more. Lalande—Lemaire," he cried
fiercely, as he held the empty shell as if about
to hurl it, "France shall be free, and so shall
Rivière!"

"No!" exclaimed Lemaire, fiercely, "not
so!"

"What!" said the others in a breath.

"France shall be free, but Rivière shall die."

"And why?"

"Because he is a traitor."

"Pish! my friend—you hate him for some reason."

"Let that be as it may," said Lemaire; "listen here. Rivière escaped to Paris—Rivière was taken again—Rivière is free! What does that mean?"

"My faith, how should I know?" asked D'Aulnay, contemptuously.

"I will tell you," said Lemaire, in a hoarse voice. "Rivière is seeking his revenge upon us for his incarceration. He is on our track—in the pay of the police."

The others started now.

"You dream," said D'Aulnay.

"Wait and see," said Lemaire. "You shall judge. I tell you he is a spy in the pay of the French police, and on our track—watching us.

He was at rendezvous after rendezvous but a few days back."

"And where is he now?" said Lalande, with eyebrows and moustache bristling.

"In the next street."

CHAPTER II.

"I MUST NOT TELL."

"OH, Dick, how dare you!" exclaimed Lady Lawler, whose cheeks were crimson. "What does this mean? Why, that poor Monsieur Rivière has been taken ill, and I could not ring for the servants. Come here!"

"I'll see you—"

"Come here, Dick," cried her ladyship, more loudly.

Sir Richard Lawler, looking very ugly and vindictive, came there.

"Now pick poor Monsieur Rivière up, and lay him on that couch."

Sir Richard strode so fiercely forward to effect the task that his lady arrested him.

"Stop!" she cried, loudly, and he stopped. "Now," she said, looking him determinedly in the face, "lift him up, Dick, gently, and without hurting him, and lay him down softly. If you do it roughly, Dick, I'll give such a shriek as will bring all the servants up to see what's the matter."

Sir Richard Lawler passed his hand over his forehead, which was rather damp, and he exhaled his breath in that half-whistle best expressed by the word "Phew!" Then, as obedient as a big boy, he placed one hand under Rivière's back and the other beneath his legs, and lifted him easily to the couch, where Lady Lawler punched and arranged the pillows for his reception.

The poor fellow sank down amongst the soft cushions with a sigh of content; while Lady Lawler button-holed her husband with a hooked finger of the left hand, and led him to the other end of the room, behind the couch; then shaking her right forefinger in his face, she said, in a half-whisper, and with a shake of her head—

"Ugh! How dare you look at me like that, sir? Dick, if we were alone, I'd box both your ears."

Sir Richard growled out something unintelligible, all but two words, and those were—

"Head—shoulder!"

"Pshaw!" ejaculated Lady Lawler, contemptuously. "But I've found it out now, Dick—I know it; and I was such a brute that I could not see it before. Poor man, he's faint for want of food."

"For want of kicking out of the house," growled Sir Richard.

"Dick, make him drink a glass of wine," said his wife, imperiously.

Sir Richard slowly filled the glass, after rinsing it out with sherry, and pouring the rinsings into the flower vase. Then he held it up to the light, smelt it, and drank it with gusto, as if he needed something to calm his perturbed spirit. Then he once more went through the rinsing process, filled the glass, and raising Rivière, held it to his lips.

After a few moments, Rivière slowly drank the wine, sank back, and then raised himself.

"I am better," he said, apologetically, and with a weary, sad look in his face that disarmed Sir Richard. "It was weak and foolish of me, but I was not well. You will excuse it, miladi— Sir Richard? A biscuit? Yes, I thank you."

He sat eating the biscuit for a few minutes, and then rose, saying—

"I am much better now. It was a strange end to our lesson, Lady Lawler; but we will do better another time."

"Oh, yes, of course," said his pupil. "You were too poorly to give it this morning, and I did not see. But you will come on Friday?"

Rivière was silent.

"Of course you will come on Friday," repeated Lady Lawler. "Richard," she cried, with a half-stamp of her foot, "ask Monsieur Rivière to be sure and come on Friday."

"Yes, to be sure," said the baronet. "You'll be sure and come on Friday?"

Rivière looked doubtfully from one to the other, till Lady Lawler came forward and placed her hand in his.

"You must come on Friday, Monsieur Rivière," she said; and he started as she spoke—for the act was so delicately done that he was taken by surprise—for, as Lady Lawler pressed his hand, it was to leave in it a couple of sovereigns.

What should he do? Refuse them? Give them back indignantly? His first wish was to do so, for it was repugnant to his feelings to have to take money from these friends; but he recalled the fact the next moment that, though generously paid, this was the wage that he had earned, and that he had a right to it; that he must take it for Marie's sake, for were they not very poor?

"Yes, I will come on Friday," said Rivière,

rising; "and I will not be weak and ill like this, Sir Richard. I thank you both much for your kindness."

He turned abruptly, and left the room; for he was still weak, and he did not wish it to be seen. In fact, he had to stop twice on the staircase to dash away the tears that would come. He managed to hide them at last, and strode out of the great house, feeling light-hearted and joyous; for had he not earned money? did he not possess the means of living?

His bright sky became overcast, though, before he had half crossed the square, for he felt that there was charity mingled with the payment. Yes, there was charity in the generous remuneration. But, after all, it was Lady Lawler's generosity, and she was rich. It was a friendly act, and there was no need for him to refuse.

"She is a noble woman," he muttered as he went on, "in spite of her weaknesses. Yes, she is weak; but then is it not given to all women to be weak? Were they not weak, they could not be so sweet, and soft, and gentle. But there, Marie, my child! you need not fear—I am thine only. Yet, for your sake, I must not tell you that I have been."

CHAPTER III.

SECRECY.

"AH! ce n'est que le premier pas qui coute," Rivière might have said. He had never before had a secret from his wife, and now he had many. He had to make excuses—inventions as to how he obtained the money which he brought home; but he could not but exult as he saw how the comforts he was able to procure brought back colour to Marie's cheek and fresh lustre to her eyes. For awhile Rivière was always on the watch for Lemaire; but the watch was in vain, and after a time he began to grow more careless, setting his dread down to imagination. Then came a time when at night he fancied he caught a glimpse of a figure gazing up at their windows, and felt sure that it was his enemy; but pursuit was in vain, or he found himself face to face with a perfect stranger.

As for Marie, she shivered at times, but by degrees grew more confident as the time glided on, and nothing in the shape of molestation occurred. They both began to feel too that they were living under laws that would be an ægis under whose protection they could rest peacefully and secure.

And so the weeks passed on, Madame Rivière still being in ignorance that her husband went regularly to the Lawlers' to give French lessons, after which Lady Lawler always insisted upon his staying to lunch, and fre-

quently to read to her from some light French
work if she felt indisposed for carriage exer-
cise.

At such times, too, the little boy used to
brought down into the drawing-room, where
Rivière would make a great fuss over him,
amusing and talking to him ; ready to yield,
too, to all his little whims and vagaries—not
a few, as may be supposed, in a child whose
every wish was constantly gratified.

"He does frighten me so, though, Monsieur
Rivière," said Lady Lawler, upon one occasion.
"Did you ever see such a boy to climb? He
is never happy unless he is up on the chairs,
and trying to get on the table."

"It is the charming vivacity of his nature,"
said Rivière, with a smile. "Nature gives it
to him that he may grow and strengthen at
every turn. He is a little angel!"

It was at this turn of the conversation that
Master Clive made a dive at his flatterer's
face, and succeeded in getting a good firm hold

of the visitor's moustache, which appendage he
did not forget to pull.

Lady Lawler smiled, called the child
" naughty baby," to get a few inarticulate
cries in reply, for Master Clive was rather back-
ward in his speech; fortunately though for
Rivière, the boy relinquished his hold, for the
owner of the moustache to smooth it softly
with a long, thin finger.

Here Jane was summoned to bear the rebel
away, and this was done, but not without a
tolerable noise and a few grabs being made
at the maiden's hair.

Sir Richard had protested against Rivière's
visits until he had been snapped into silence,
and of late he had been more accustomed to
his yoke. He set it down to his wife's whim
with respect to acquiring French; and, avoiding as often as was possible all encounters with
Rivière, he was to a great extent saved from
the angry feelings which would have been
sure to arise on seeing the lavish attention

paid by Rivière, and the evident satisfaction
evinced at the offered incense on the other
side.

It took time; but Rivière grew at last to
look upon Lady Lawler in her true light—that
of a vain woman fond of flattery; and he paid
his court accordingly, attended with due regularity, gave lessons when Lady Lawler was
disposed to receive them, and when she was not,
read until requested to desist on the plea that
he must be very tired. The pleasant fiction of
various pupils was kept up in Soho; and after
the first few weeks Marie religiously abstained
from mentioning the name of Grosvenor-square,
firmly believing all the while that its existence
was nearly forgotten by her husband.

It was with a certain amount of uneasiness
that upon two occasions Rivière, after an hour
spent in a neighbouring café, mounted to
his humble apartments. Upon each of these
days he had met a man who he felt sure must
be Lemaire; and now his uneasiness increased

as he felt the possibility that his fancied security had all been false, and that while he had been away from home and perfectly at ease, it was possible that his rooms had been watched, and even that some conspiracy was hatching against his peace.

But was this man that he had met Lemaire? The contour was the same; the peculiar look, too, in the eyes; but he was sufficiently well disguised to make Rivière doubt his identity. Had he met him with a bold, defiant look, all doubt would have been at an end; but the man had passed him with a heavy, apathetic stare, which mystified him until he reached home, where the anxious, troubled look upon his wife's face brought back the suspicion with redoubled force.

" Has any one been here?" he said, peering eagerly in her face.

" Been here? No," Madame Rivière replied. " Why do you ask?"

Rivière made no direct answer, but muttered

something about business matters, and turned
off the question.

Upon the second occasion of his encounter
in the streets, the suspicion that he felt grew
stronger. He was convinced that Lemaire had
been to the house in his absence, and he felt
that the fact was being kept from him, evidently
from a dread of something worse happening
should he know.

However, he dissembled, and hid his annoyance; but all the time the thought he harboured
grew and grew, so that it troubled him more
than he could have told.

It was not the first time that he had allowed
suspicion to enter his breast, and the recollection of its former injustice ought to have
been sufficient to drive it forth ; but at this time
Rivière, though with what he considered good
intentions, was engaged in a systematic course
of deceit, and himself deceiving, he was too
ready to accuse others. The practice of one
deception acted as a canker, and its poison

spread, so that he proceeded to do the first thing which occurred to his mind—that was to watch; and he watched stealthily day after day, both going to and coming from his little home, but without effect.

CHAPTER IV.

MEPHISTOPHELES.

ATTERS had been going on smoothly for some time at Grosvenor-square.

The servants had been talking and making such remarks as they pleased; but apparently Sir Richard had allowed things to drift, and, yielding to the supremacy of his lady, growled mentally, but said nothing.

Rivière set off to give the lesson one morning, not in the best of tempers, for it had struck him that Marie was cold and distant.

"Where are you going?" she had said.

"Oh, only to give a lesson—some people in the west."

Madame ˌRivière said nothing; but her eyes flashed as she turned away and recalled for the hundredth time the fact that he had not told her where he went with such regularity. She suspected now; but she would not ask—she could not watch. No; he should tell her himself, or she would bear all in silence. That wicked woman!

This applied to Lady Lawler, whose bold, handsome face was ever rising before her in such times of trouble, like the evil genius of her existence. But ever as she suspected that her husband visited at Grosvenor-square, she became more self-contained, and determined to keep her thoughts to herself.

No pleasant state of affairs when husband and wife are suspicious one of the other, and with some ground for their suspicion.

Rivière had not been gone very long before Marie rose, very stern and thoughtful of aspect, dressed, and went out to provide some few necessaries wanted for their domestic use.

It was not the first time, and she was not
surprised to find that before she had gone a
hundred yards some one was walking close
behind her; and she did not start as a voice
said, in a tone just loud enough for her to
hear—

" I see you then once again."

Madame Rivière did not answer.

" Have you attended to that which I begged
and prayed of you to do?"

No reply—no motion on the part of Madame
Rivière to show that she heard a word.

" Heaven! that an angel should be made the
slave of one who lives to deceive her!"

Still no notice taken; only Marie Rivière's
lips were set very firmly as she walked steadily
on, without even increasing her pace.

" But I might have known that you were too
good and trusting to disbelieve. You would
not credit it if I went down here upon my
knees in the open street and swore that he
had an assignation in Grosvenor-square—that

he has gone there regularly ever since you left."

Still silence, only that after a minute Marie heard a deep sigh. Then her follower spoke again—

"You do not believe it?"

Here they were opposite a shop where Marie had a commission to perform; and as she entered, still without a trace of emotion upon her handsome pale face, Monsieur Lemaire, looking sleek, dark, and treacherous as a cat waiting to make a spring, walked slowly on for a few yards before turning, and then walking back as far on the other side of the shop, kept up a regular sentry march, as if guarding a prisoner, till he saw Madame Rivière come quietly out and continue her journey.

He was at her side as she passed, and she heard him sigh; but he might have been invisible, so utterly did she ignore his presence, and walk slowly on.

"Can I do nothing to prove my faith and truth?"

No answer; though the words were almost breathed into her ear, as she walked on without hastening a step.

"You will not believe me?"

Madame Rivière paused for a moment, apparently attracted by something in a shop they were passing, and Lemaire seized the opportunity to whisper—

"Will you see, and judge for yourself?"

Madame Rivière was satisfied with her glance at the shop window, and passed on.

"It is for your own sake I ask it. Indeed, indeed it is."

Then he went on earnestly—

"I have long learned to bear in silence the scorn with which you treat me. Had I been a dog, you could not have been more cruel; but I bear all—everything in silence, as my fate, and I do not murmur. For myself all is past; but it maddens me when I see you—you so beautiful, a woman who should be worshipped with all a lover's mad idolatry, systematically cheated, deceived, your sweet, pure, womanly affection slighted, trampled under foot; and all for the sake of that vile, meretricious creature, who sits in diamonds to-day to meet him, while her poor, weak, deluded husband looks on in silence."

There was not a change in the expression of Marie Rivière's countenance. It was still very pale, and her lips were pressed closely together. One who knew her well might perhaps have detected that her thin, fine nostrils were slightly dilated; but even that might have been the result of the walk.

Now, basket in hand, she stepped into another shop, and came out—Lemaire still sentry at the door. Another shop, and a few more purchases —Lemaire still sentry.

This time the last commission was fulfilled, and Madame Rivière turned her steps homeward, with the black shadow of her life once more closely behind.

"I have watched for days that I might say this," he said, as he walked now at her shoulder. "You would not notice my letters; but I was obliged to tell you. Oh, Marie, Marie!— cannot you believe that I would die for your sake?"

The wayfarers were many here, and no words were spoken. Then, once again—

"Pray watch for yourself, and you will find that I have not deceived you. I ask no recompense, only that you will believe I do this for the sake of the woman I have always madly loved, and who never can be mine. For I worship you, Marie, for your truth and goodness; for your fidelity to one who deserves it not; and my compensation is to think of what might have been had it been otherwise."

Nearer home now; and Lemaire, while he walked so closely and whispered his poison in her ear, evidently watchfully on the lookout.

"In another few moments my life will again be blank," he murmured; "but do not let my words be treated heedlessly. Seek this out. Reproach him and bring him back to your side; for it is for your happiness I am now concerned. Only let me see your heart at peace, and I shall be content. What greater recompense could I desire? Name it."

There was only opportunity for a few more words, and Lemaire was not slow to use it.

"You treat me with scorn and contempt, but I bear it—I have even grown to love it. And look here, Marie, it is unspeakable joy to me to be your slave; and that I am, come what may. You do not believe me now; but you will find out that I am no liar—no defamer of the character of Louis Rivière. When you have satisfied yourself upou these points, you will want help. You will wish to return to fair, sunny France. Come to me then for aid. Let me see you safely back in your own

country, and then send me away—back here, if
you will. Banish me from your sight for ever;
but let me know that I have been of some slight
service to you, if but once in my life."

Lemaire had timed his words well. As he
finished, Marie Rivière crossed the road and
walked into the open doorway of the house
where they lived. She had kept up well:
neither by gesture nor countenance could
Lemaire have told that she had heard a word;
but his eyes twinkled strangely from beneath
his half-closed lids as he saw her pass slowly
out of his sight, when he, too, disappeared,
smiling and thoughtful, as he made his way
towards the house where he knew the con-
spirators were holding a meeting. And by
intuition he could tell something of what was
going on in Marie Rivière's room. He more
than suspected that it had been by a tremendous effort of self-control that she had
listened apparently unmoved to all that he had
said. For as he slowly walked away, the poor

woman, with trembling knees, climbed to her room, closed the door, and, sobbing hysterically, threw herself upon her knees to bury her face in the bed, and moan as if her suffering were greater than she could bear.

CHAPTER V.

A STORM.

MEANWHILE Rivière had reached Grosvenor - square, where he was shown into the drawing - room, to find Lady Lawler dressed and about to go out.

"Ah, Monsieur Rivière, I am so glad you have come," she exclaimed. "I was just going for a drive."

As she spoke she rang the bell.

"Tell Edwards I shall not want the carriage," she said to the servant who answered her summons; and the man went out with a grin upon his face, which he further distorted by thrusting his tongue into one cheek—entirely, though, for his own edification.

"Yes, I'm so glad you have come," said Lady Lawler again. "Sir Richard has gone down into the country for three days, so we can have plenty of reading."

"But miladi will go out," said Rivière; "I will come again. Do not let the carriage be kept back."

"Oh, no," said Lady Lawler, smiling. "I can have the carriage at any time, when I cannot have a lesson. See what a good pupil you have. There, come and take a chair," she continued, seating herself; "and bring that with you."

She pointed to a French novel, and upon its being brought, she read about a couple of pages, after which she complained of hoarseness.

"There, Monsieur Rivière, you must read now," she said, throwing herself back in a fauteuil; and, taking the book, Rivière read on patiently for quite a couple of hours.

Then it seemed for the first time to occur to her ladyship that the reader might be just a little fatigued—an impeachment that Rivière, of course, denied.   However, she rang for sherry and biscuits, after partaking of which Rivière rose to leave.

"You will be sure and come to-morrow?" said Lady Lawler.

"Do you wish it?" said Rivière.   "Will you not have visits to pay?"

"Oh, no; you need not fear that.   Pray come. You will, will you not?"

"I am miladi's slave," said Rivière, gallantly.

He took the extended hand, held it for a moment, and then, as if urged by an after-thought, pressed it to his lips, while the weak woman flushed slightly with pleasure, and then started; for before Rivière had completed his old school salutation, Sir Richard Lawler, looking flushed and angry, strode rapidly over the soft carpet which hushed his footsteps, and, with an oath, struck the Frenchman so furious a blow that he staggered back against a side table, over-setting and breaking a great vase which stood thereon.

Lady Lawler seemed to lose her self-control, for she shrieked wildly, and tore at the bell; while, white with passion, Rivière recovered himself, sprang up, and darted at his assailant, who received him with a heavy blow full in the chest, which again sent him staggering back; for Sir Richard had been losing at the country race he had attended, and had come back suddenly, much flushed with wine.

Alarmed by the shrieks and furious bell-ringing, three of the servants now rushed into the room, to stare aghast at so unusual a scene in a gentleman's drawing-room.

For a moment or two Rivière leaned breathless and panting against a table, whose ornaments were plunged into wild confusion; then, small and weak as he was, he once more made at his muscular, burly aggressor, whose hoarse voice was now loudly heard.

"Here, Sellars, Williams, James, throw this scoundrel down the stairs—kick him out of the house!"

"Back, canaille!" exclaimed Rivière, with flashing eyes, as the servants approached; and there was that in his appearance which thoroughly kept them at bay, even though they were three to one.

"Do you hear me?" roared Sir Richard to his men.

"Yes, they hear you," hissed Rivière; "but now you shall hear me. Sir Richard Lawler, you have insulted me affreusement. I demand satisfaction."

"Satisfaction?" cried Sir Richard, mockingly. "You dog! Think yourself lucky, you treacherous hound, that I don't horsewhip you."

"Horsewhip me? You are mad!" said Rivière, speaking very slowly, but in a cold, cutting voice, while the glaring of his eyes and his extreme pallor showed the passion which was kept down by a tremendous effort. "Sir," he half whispered, "I ask for satisfaction. I am a gentleman, sir—for satisfaction."

"Am I to speak again?" roared Sir Richard, ignoring Rivière, and scowling at his servants. "Out with the scoundrel at once!"

He then crossed to the bell, and tore at it furiously; for Lady Lawler, after trying vainly to make herself heard, had turned pale with alarm, and sunk fainting upon a chair.

"Back, canaille!" exclaimed Rivière, hoarsely, as the servants, urged by their master's voice, began to approach him with inimical intentions; and small as he was of stature, his waved hand and fierce look had their effect, aided possibly by the impression made on the servants' minds by the left hand, which seemed to lurk ominously within his breast.

"Them Frenchmen is so fond of the knife,"

muttered James, as he set the example of shrinking back.

And in one way or the other the servants were kept at bay, although there was nothing more fearsome in the breast pocket which Rivière searched than a card, which was so dirty from friction that he could not fling it in Sir Richard's face.

"You scoundrels!" roared the baronet, "must I do it myself?"

And he approached Rivière with flushed face and upraised hands; but the little Frenchman did not flinch, and Sir Richard stopped, confused, a couple of paces off.

"Sir Richard," said Rivière, fiercely, "you have insulted your lady here in the presence of your servants, and you have insulted me. I demand satisfaction."

"Curse you! will you put him out, or must I?" roared Sir Richard; and now, forgetting one dread in the other, the men made for Rivière, who dashed the back of his hand smartly in the face of one powdered colossus, and then, shaking his fist ominously at Sir Richard, glided rather than ran from the room.

CHAPTER VI.

A FEW VICTIMS.

N Doctor D'Aulnay's room things were as usual excessively dirty, and scrupulously clean; and the strip of wood nailed across formed the line of separation. A moderator burned upon the table, for the forge fire was just fading out; but it was evident that the occupant of the room had lately been busily at work, for various chemical vessels were standing about in disorder amongst broken glass and stands. Sand from a sand-bath was overturned and scattered about; but a couple of bottles were standing full of a powder, and carefully tied over with what seemed to be soft leather.

There had evidently, too, been work going on at the lathe, where iron had been turned. There were a dozen hemispherical cups lying on the bench, of various degrees of brightness, and the floor about sparkled with dust and tiny shavings of iron, which had evidently curled off under the hard steel tool, which had treated the iron cups as if they had been some close-grained wood in the turner's hand.

But work was over, and Doctor D'Aulnay was indulging in recreation in the clean portion of his room, amongst his flowers. He had been smoking, and the ash of a couple of cigars lay in a neat tray. He had been reading, too—a French work upon the government of nations—and the book lay open. The Doctor was evidently a thinker, and the broad margin of every page was covered with notes, written in an almost microscopic hand—original ideas of his own; and he had smiled as he added them, thinking of the regeneration of France, and the blessings he would pour down upon the land if he should ever win his way to power after blowing a few of the unworthy ones to infinitesimally small fragments by means of the ingenious shells, which were his own special invention.

But the Doctor was not reading now. He was enjoying himself in a philosophical way, for he was of opinion that time was too valuable to be wasted. He even approached the sublime in his ways of life, for even in his dreams he was busy over the regeneration of his country, and the means for improving the efficiency of his shells.

There was a wire cage upon the table where the Doctor sat, and in it a couple of sparrows, which seemed exceedingly dissatisfied with that habitation, and kept on fluttering against the bars, beating their breasts bare. In a small basket close by there was something else alive, which scratched and moved about restlessly; and on the other side—green, goggle-eyed, passive—in a basin, partly covered by a plate of common window glass, a great frog.

The philosopher's hair was black and close as ever, and threw his white forehead, marked with thin lines, into powerful contrast. His eyes were twinkling brightly, and his white teeth were set hard upon his lower lip.

There was a small stoppered bottle upon the table ; and, after sitting thinking for awhile, the Doctor took it up, removed the stopper cautiously, and then passed it rapidly beneath his nose.

It was but a momentary action, and on the instant he snatched it away and closed the stopper.

His next act was to take up a quill pen, and sharpen the point, making it long and taper. This done, he galvanised the frog into action

by taking the glass lid from the basin. Another
instant, and the wide-mouthed creature had
leaped out of the water, but into a cloth cun-
ningly placed to receive it; and in a few
moments the poor thing was swathed in what
was to be its winding-sheet, for it was wrapped
round and round until only the head was left
bare, its tormentor holding it firmly in his left
hand.

A little manipulation with an ivory book
mark, and the mouth was opened; then the
pen was dipped into the contents of the stoppered bottle, and one tiny drop dripped into
the frog's mouth, which was then permitted to
close.

The cloth was then unwound, and the object
of the experiment allowed to fall on the table,
which it did, not to leap actively about, but to
fall flaccid, and with its legs outstretched, quite
dead.

The Doctor smiled complacently, rose from
his chair, took up the unfortunate reptile by

one of its limp legs, carried it to the window, and—flip!—it was falling headlong to the hard stones far below, to be ready for the trampling hoofs of the next horse.

"Good," said D'Aulnay, smiling as he returned to the table, and prepared for his second experiment.

This was to place his hand in the cage where the sparrows fluttered; and, after a struggle, he secured one, which turned up to him its little, bead-like eyes, and panted and struggled feebly against the cruel hand. But its release was near. D'Aulnay took out the stopper from the little wide-mouthed bottle, and in its place inserted, beak downwards, the wretched sparrow's head, watching it the while with earnest, glittering eyes.

There was just room for the bird's head, the feathers closing up the sides so that but little air could get in, and at the first inspiration there was a change; at the second, a feeble struggle; then the wings grew limp, the muscles of the

neck failed to do their work, and the Doctor
threw the bird upon the table, dead.

He smiled again, evidently well satisfied; and,
taking up the bottle, the temptation seemed to
be strong upon him to hold it to his nostrils;
but he resisted the desire, and stoppered it once
more; while he took the dead sparrow to the
little forge, raised a small cake of black coal
dust, and dropped the tiny corpse into an
incandescent hole.

It was now the turn of the next sparrow,
whose fluttering was being watched by a cat
which now showed itself, crouching close to
one of the windows; but which had evidently,
from its shrinking ways, been too well taught
to allow of its making any piratical raids upon
its master's property. It looked very eager and
hungry, though, as it saw the second sparrow
caught; and, schooled as it was, it could not
refrain from giving a dismal "miouw!" and
licking its thin gums while gazing with dilated
eyes; but it made not so much as a pace

forward, but rather shrank back more into the shade, for the light upon the table left much of the room in darkness.

D'Aulnay smiled grimly as he watched the cat, and held in his hand the sparrow, which, as if dreading the worst, made a resolute stand for its life, fluttering, scratching with its claws, and digging its little hard beak furiously into its captor's hand, upon which it left red marks.

"Lie still, little beast!" said D'Aulnay, smiling as he took up a large needle, removed the stopper, plunged the needle twice in the liquid, and then, laying aside the feathers upon the poor bird's breast, punctured it once in the fleshy part, carefully avoiding the piercing of any vital organ.

Then, closing the bottle once more, and still holding the sparrow in his hand, he walked again to the furnace, and dropped the needle into the burning coal.

By the time he had reached the table again

the bird lay passive, with its little eyes half closed—quite dead.

"Here, puss!" he said, with a malicious look upon his grim face; and he threw the bird on the floor, to be seized by the cat, which retreated, growling and spitting, into a corner, but only to be driven out by the Doctor.

"Go there—under the furnace, beast!" he said. "No feathers here."

The cat evidently had a warm lurking-place in the indicated spot, and rushed there with flashing, dilated eyes, evidently in an agony of dread lest she should be deprived of her bonne bouche.

But D'Aulnay had no intention of interfering with her repast; for as soon as she had disappeared he once more returned to the table, taking with him a small piece of bright red carrot. This he set to and prepared by dipping the quill pen as before into the bottle, and then piercing the piece of carrot three or four times.

This done, he burnt the quill; and, opening the basket, took out a pretty little white rabbit by its ears, the tame little animal settling down upon the table instantly, and suffering itself to be patted and stroked while it busily munched the carrot to the last bit, when it set up its ears, shook its head, tore at its nose with its fore paws for a few moments, then gave a feeble squeak, set off as if to run, and rolled over on its side, dead.

"Good!" said the Doctor, who had been intently watching the experiment, rubbing his hands. "It is excellent, marvellous! What a power! For the enemies of La France that cannot be reached with shells. Let me see," he said, grimly, and counting upon his fingers; "by direct action; by inhalation; by puncture; by indirect action—Ah! what is this?"

He was startled by a wild yell from the unfortunate cat, another victim, though not intended; for she now rushed from the hole beneath the furnace, careered furiously round the room, and in another instant would have been amongst the bottles.

The Doctor turned ghastly, crouched like a wild beast, and seemed as if about at all hazards to leap from the window; for he knew the effect of a breakage amongst his deadly preparations. But he was safe; for as the cat gathered itself up for a spring which would have landed her amongst the receptacles of the poudre d'enfer, her muscles relaxed, and with a dismal moan she fell prone—dead.

"Ah!" said the Doctor, smiling, and drawing a longer breath, as he wiped the dew from his forehead. "Ah—yes—decidedly by indirect action; one that cannot be touched by water."

Then he stood thoughtfully nodding his head for a few moments before glancing at his watch.

"Ah!" he exclaimed; "so late! They will be here."

Hurriedly putting away the bottle, he next thrust open the window, seized the cat by the

tail, gave it a good swing, and sent his victim
far away into the street, listening till he heard it
come down with a dull thud.

" No one will eat that," he said, grimly ;
" and the sweepers will soon take it away, unless
some one takes it up for the skin : if so, let him
beware. But that is his affair, not mine. Now
for the rabbit."

This shared the fate of one sparrow; for
making a hole in the black cake of coal, the
little white animal was thrust into its fiery
grave, and a shovel of coal dust being added,
the working of the bellows for a few minutes
calcined the ill-fated little animal; and the
Doctor washed his hands.

"What a beautifully clean thing is fire," he
said, softly. "So is water," he added, after a
pause. "Ah, here come my friends. Vive la
France!"

Steps were heard upon the stairs; and, throwing open the door, he held up the lamp to light
the way for Hippolyte Lalande and Lemaire,

who came in with another man, who was saluted by the Doctor as Fevre.

"It is time, I suppose?" said D'Aulnay, interrogatively.

Lemaire nodded.

"You have no doubts?" said D'Aulnay.

"Ask the others," said Lemaire. "You think me partial."

The Doctor turned to Lalande.

"Not a doubt," said the latter. "But come and judge for yourself."

"And you?" said the Doctor, turning to the new-comer.

"Come and see," said Fevre. "I have no doubts."

"And that English milord who was in France?"

"He is a fool," said Lemaire; "but his wife is with them, and leads the husband too. He has influence, and if steps are not taken to frighten them, we shall even be hunted from here. The police are very watchful already. It is evident that something is on the way."

"Then we must strike the first blow," exclaimed D'Aulnay, fiercely. "It is for La France."

"Yes; for La France," said the others, excepting Lemaire, who remained silent.

"And those English in Grosvenor-square?" said Fevre.

"One at a time," said D'Aulnay. "There are ways and ways of striking. The secret is to be cautious, and not to try too much at once."

"You have reason," said Lalande; "and now, gentlemen, are you ready?"

Lemaire's response was to begin covering the lower part of his face so as to form a disguise.

"You are silent, Monsieur Lemaire," said D'Aulnay.

"I am a suspect," said the former, meaningly. "You say I have enmity, and work for my own aims. Perhaps so. Anyhow, I am with you in this expedition."

"Good," said D'Aulnay, laying his hand upon the lamp after assuming his hat; "and now, gentlemen, are you ready?"

"Yes," was the reply, as with one voice.

And they stole softly out of the room, closely followed by D'Aulnay, who only paused to turn down the lamp, and then to lock and transfer to his pocket the key of his door.

CHAPTER VII.

FULL OF DOUBT.

TWO hours' hard walking to and fro upon the green sward in Hyde Park hardly sufficed to cool down the first ebullitions of the Frenchman's anger. He had torn his hair, stamped and gesticulated until he had attracted the attention of a policeman, who had come up and surlily announced that "they had had enough of that," and advised him to move on.

So Rivière strode hastily away to another part of the park, where he recommenced his angry striding up and down. He would have satisfaction, that he would. There should be a meeting. The baronet's had been a most gross insult, and he should encounter him. Yes, he was a gentleman. His faith, that such a gross rough boor should be a gentleman! He should meet him. He would tell him that he had cruelly maligned Lady Lawler. No, he would not tell him that. Lady Lawler was a woman who could fight her own battles, and she would teach him to dare to make aspersions on her character. A cur—a pig! How dare he indulge in his base suspicions?

Rivière smiled grimly as he thought of Lady Lawler's spirit, and the power she possessed over her husband. Sir Richard would not dare to meet him; he would not be allowed, but he would have to make an humble apology. Yes, it would be sent him in the morning, with a request from Lady Lawler that he would return.

The baronet must have been drunk—mad with losses, or something. Yes, Lady Lawler would be writing; but Marie must not see the letter, or she would learn where his lessons were given. But did she know now?

He was cooling down fast. He would accept the apology for Marie's sake; but he could go to Grosvenor-square no more; and he must seek in earnest now for other pupils.

First, to return home. Was he sufficiently calm? He thought so now; and he walked along, down street after street, to soothe the irritation of his feelings.

A glance or two in different shop windows had shown him that the only visible traces of his past encounter were the starting veins in his temples, and by degrees they beat less furiously. And now he began to ponder about sending a friend to wait upon the baronet. It was awkward; for he had no friends now. But he must find some one who would be his second. It would doubtless be easy, for there were plenty in Soho who would support the honour of La France.

Suppose he fell! What would become of Marie? And, on the other hand, suppose he killed the Englishman, how could he face his gentle, confiding wife? But his honour—he had been struck. There was no evasion—the Englishman must apologize.

With these musings flitting through his brain, Rivière's pace grew more rapid, and he avoided the wayfarers as if by instinct, seeing nothing till, crossing Wardour-street and entering Soho-square by a narrow dingy way, he became aware once more of the figure which he supposed to be Lemaire's issuing from the street where his own lodging was situated.

He started at once in pursuit, determined to examine well the features of this cause of un-easiness; but, before he could reach him, he saw him turn a corner, and by the time Rivière reached that he was gone—had entered, perhaps, one of the thirty or forty houses with open doors on either side—perhaps passed on; who could say?

Rivière's brow knit, and the veins began to start out once more by his temples, as a shiver of dread and jealousy swept through him; and in spite of himself he began to make comparisons between himself and Sir Richard, and he thought at last of what would have been his own feelings had he returned home and been witness of such a scene as had met the baronet's eye.

"But I am a fool," he muttered, as he wiped the dew from his forehead. "I will be open and plain with Marie; and as for her, poor child, she would not receive a visitor without telling me. No, no—she is too ingenuous, too pure."

Nevertheless, his first question upon entering the room where Madame Rivière was at work took this form—

"Has any one been?"

"Been—here? No," said Marie, glancing sharply at him. "Why do you ask?"

"Because—I fancied some one might have called."

Husband and wife were not at one, for the same thought was in each breast—

"Why should anything be kept back?"

Marie sat working and watching her husband furtively for some time; while he, rejecting the frugal meal prepared for him amidst temptations he did not suspect, sat with his head resting on his hand, moody and thoughtful, as he passed before him in array his day's adventures.

About this meeting. That was the question —how was it to be brought about? He must find a friend. It must be at one of the cafés; but it was hard to know in whom to confide. Anyhow, the matter must be gone about carefully, or else this Englishman might take advantage of his country's customs and hand him over to the police, charging him with attempting to break the peace, and binding him over in sums of money and sureties. What complications would this produce, for to whom could he fly to be his bondsmen?

Yes—he knew enough of English habits and customs to feel that he was right here, and that the task must be delicately adventured upon; so he determined to sleep upon it.

The next day found him as hot as ever against Sir Richard; and going to a neighbouring café, from which he dated the missive, he sent the baronet a fiercely indited letter, inviting him to give the name of a friend.

That day, after his letter was sent, he spent going from café to café and estaminet about Soho, attentively watching the various faces of the inmates, till first one and then another would slowly rise and leave the place.

This took place several times, but Rivière did not notice it, for his mind was bent upon one object — to find a compatriot, a gentleman, who would be his second in the coming encounter.

Quite late at night he sat at the café where he had written his note, almost alone; for, still unperceived by Rivière, his presence had had the same strange effect: first one and then another habitué had turned, and seen him watching his countenance, and becoming uneasy had risen and left the place, till the garçon had ejaculated as he removed half-finished cups of coffee, and gathered together the loose dominoes lying upon the little marble tables. Such behaviour was unaccountable.

It was too soon, perhaps, to expect a reply— that night, it was the very earliest season ; so after staying quite late, he rose and left the café, not hearing the exclamation of the garçon, who, used to very quiet and careful customers as he was, found Rivière an exception.

"Four hours, and only one cup of coffee !" he muttered, raising his hands.

Then, strolling slowly towards the door, he stood looking after Rivière, to become the next moment all animation, for a man passed him closely, gave him a meaning look, and laid one finger on his lips.

"Aha !" he said softly. "What means this ?"

He gazed down the gaslit street, and saw
Rivière slowly walking on the other side.
Gazing attentively, he could make out that
there was a man about ten paces in front,
another about as far behind, and two on the
other side of the road—the latter of whom
was the one who had laid his finger upon his
lips.

He stood watching them for about a couple
of minutes, when the last figure became indis-
tinct, as it passed a lamp-post far down the
street. Then he stooped lower, and stood with
one hand over his ear, listening attentively.

"What is it, Jules?" said a voice at his side;
and he turned to face his proprietor, at whom
he gazed meaningly.

"Listen, we shall hear something."

"A spy?" whispered the proprietor, interrogatively.

"My faith, yes, I think so. Ah, cursed
brigand!" he exclaimed shaking his fist at the
driver of a cab, who urged his horse with a

great deal of rattle and noise down the narrow street.

"There are the police, too," whispered the proprietor. "It will not be to-night."

CHAPTER VIII.

CAUGHT IN A TRAP.

RIVIERE, meanwhile, had sauntered slowly along the street, perfectly unaware of the fact that he was the object of so much attention, and that, irrespective of his own suspicious behaviour in going into the haunts of and watching men who were for the most part proscribed and leagued together in plots against the ruling powers of their own country, he had a powerful enemy at work against him. In fact, for days past he had never left his home unwatched; but it had been performed in so quiet and careful a way that he was in the most profound ignorance of the fact. Even had his mind been less occupied by thoughts of Lemaire and Sir Richard Lawler, it is doubtful whether he would have perceived it, so cleverly had it been managed.

Doubts had been felt by more than one at first, for Lemaire was not popular amongst them, and it was guessed that he was working for his own ends; but, unfortunately for Rivière, his later acts swept away all doubts. It was only too evident that he was a spy—a clumsy and a bungling spy, working for the Louis Philippe Government; and at more than one conference it had been decided that, with the plans they had on hand, a spy could not be tolerated in their midst.

As Rivière sauntered along, it almost seemed as if he were inviting molestation; or was he so well armed that he could set those who followed him at defiance? He must have friends within call.

Were things shaping themselves to work ill

for Louis Rivière? It never rains but it pours, says the old proverb. He must either be inadvertently doing everything possible to increase suspicion into something beyond doubt, or else be really a spy; for now he stopped in front of another café, and, raising himself on tiptoe, peered over the blind, and gazed into the almost empty room.

As he gazed in, the man on the opposite side of the street walked a dozen yards past the lamp-post and crossed over. The others, too, drew nearer, and were all now pretty close; but Rivière did not heed them. He stepped back to the pavement and walked slowly on, muttering—

" He is not there."

Then he stopped for a moment, as if undecided, ending by walking on pretty sharply now, though the next street was that where his apartments were.

He had nearly reached the door, unaware of the fact that a shawl-draped form was leaning, anxiously watching, from an upper window, when a man before him stopped, hesitated, and then turned to and addressed him in French.

" Would monsieur direct him to Philip-street ? "

"Certainly. It was the second turning to the right, then the third to the left, and again the second to the right."

But, his faith, he was confused. He was strange in the dreadful wilderness of a London —so different from dear Paris. He had wandered and lost himself. If monsieur would accept a cigar, and show him ?

Rivière hesitated instinctively for a few moments. He knew not why, but it was as if some internal monitor had whispered, "Take care!" Then laughing to himself, he took the proffered cigar with a few words of thanks, lit it from that of the stranger—the two men, as they stood face to face, puffing at the small rolls of tobacco, lighting up in flashes each the other's face; and as Rivière glanced for a moment in the other's eyes, he again felt the same instinctive feeling of shrinking dread.

He shook it off, though, the next moment, saying—

"I am at monsieur's service. It is pleasant to aid a compatriot on these sombre shores."

"Ah, yes—sombre shores indeed," said the other, walking side by side with Rivière. "The place is sad—so sad! One never feels joyous here—one rarely smiles. How do these islanders live? What streets! Look at this: how gloomy! No boulevards—no little tables where one can sit and sip one's eau sucrée or black coffee. No places where one can have a petit verre. Nought but great public-houses, where the barbarians drink beer from great metal pots, and fearful women drink gin—what they call blue ruin. It is a fearful place!"

"This turning," said Rivière, who listened while his companion volubly chattered on.

He would have turned back and left the stranger to find his own way, only it seemed absurd; and, besides, had he not accepted his cigar? What was there to mind? This man could have no connection with Lemaire. His troubles were turning his brain.

All the same, though, as the stranger chattered away, Rivière noticed now for the first time that a man was walking a few paces in front, and that he took, as if intuitively, precisely the same route as that they themselves pursued.

"Let him," laughed Rivière to himself. "What matters? I have neither money nor watch. But stay!"

He shivered, for it suddenly occurred to him that it might be possible that the French police had emissaries even in London. But he pooh-poohed it the next moment, and answered a question from his new-found friend.

"Were there good theatres in London?"

"Oh, yes, he believed so; but he had not seen much of them. This turning."

What turns—what a maze! He was monsieur's debtor for ever. He would never have found his way alone; but have had to pass the night walking up and down those deplorable, dingy streets, every one of which was enough to give any one the spleen.

But he might have asked the police—there is one.

To be sure, yes. What folly! The police would have helped him, of course. What, another turn?

Yes, another turn; and, as they took it, Rivière glanced sharply round, to see the policeman they had passed had done precisely the same thing, and was watching them. He saw more—namely, that two men were a short distance behind. Then, going on, he saw the other man was in front.

Another street, the stranger still chattering in the most lively way; and now Rivière glanced back once more. There were the two men behind, and there was one in front. But they had only another street to go down, and there was Philip-street.

The long rows of houses looked very dark and dingy, with only a light here and there at very wide distances; for the hour was late. The gas lamps stood at the customary stations; but they only blinked dismally, and shed but little light. There was a cold chill in the air, it seemed to Rivière, and he was anxious to get away and hurry home; but he would see it through now. And besides, what of those other men who followed them? Bah! it was childish. He was nervous and unhinged.

He glanced round once more.

"Is anything wrong that you look back?" said the stranger.

"I don't like those men following us," said Rivière, in a low voice.

"Mon Dieu! but I hope there is no danger," said the stranger, catching at Rivière's arm. "Shall we go back to the police?"

" Oh, no," said Rivière, smiling, "it was perhaps only a silly suspicion; and besides, you are safe —we are here."

"Ah, yes, it is good. This is Philip-street, and my house—my lodgment is—my faith, which is it? How different it is by night. Is monsieur sure, though, that this is Philip-street?"

"Yes, and make haste," said Rivière, in low, sharp tones. "Which is your number? These men are closing in upon us."

"Heavens, what a position!" exclaimed the stranger, speaking in short, husky tones. "But, yes," he exclaimed, joyfully, "I had forgotten the number, but that is the house. I know it by that head over the door. It is good—we now have refuge if those men mean us wrong. We are here."

It was a dark street of the region of dark streets, and by the flickering gaslights looked unusually forbidding. Late as was the hour, several doors, whose posts were ornamented with an abundant crop of bell handles, stood open. It was at one of these that the stranger halted.

"Thank Heaven!" he exclaimed; "but those

men! It looks very suspicious; they have evidently some design. Ah, this London!"

Rivière saw, too, on the instant that these three
men evidently had some design; for as he stood
in front of the open door, with his hand raised
to his hat, he saw the first man stop short and
turn round, and the others closing up.

Yes, there was some design in this; and
Rivière's hands clenched: so did his teeth, biting
right through the cigar, the lighted portion of
which fell to the ground.

"I see what to do," whispered the stranger.
"I am safe, but I cannot leave you to your fate.
You will come in with me—to my room—till
they have gone by; or you can watch from the
window for a police, and he will see you home.
To be sure, come in."

There seemed to be nothing else to do, always
supposing that these silent men, closing in so
quickly now, had inimical ideas. Unless, indeed, he should determine to dash through them,
and run until a policeman came in sight. It was

a strange position—in busy London, too; but the streets were deserted, and Rivière had not many moments for choice. He saw on the instant that which his companion whispered, laying a hand upon his arm—

"Here, quick; it is your only chance—they are thieves, and are after you. In, quick, and I will bang to the door."

The decoy bird had done his part well, and without a suspicion Rivière took his first step into the dark passage. Ere he took the second he knew that he had been betrayed.

It was but the work of a few seconds. As he darted in, he felt himself seized, and his arms pinned to his side. A cry was at his lips, when something thick was over his head, and he felt that he was being dragged down by many hands. He could hear hard breathing and trampling feet, and the boards creaked as he struggled fiercely for his liberty—for aught he knew, for his life. Then a sharp cry seemed to pierce the air, sounding muffled and strange though; and it seemed to him that the cry was his—that he had uttered it in his despair. Then all seemed misty and strange, his head swam, he felt sick and giddy, and he knew no more.

CHAPTER IX.

SAVED FOR THIS ONCE.

UT Rivière had not seen the dark shawled figure that was leaning out of the window of his lodging, and did not know that that figure, after listening eagerly for such words as she could catch of the conversation that took place at the door, came down hastily and followed cautiously upon the track of those who had gone before.

For Marie Rivière was ill at ease. She

doubted her husband. She felt convinced that he went to the Lawlers', and that he had deceived her upon that point; but was he not her husband still, and should she not, as far as in her lay, watch over him and guard him from all evil? There was danger abroad, she was sure of that. Lemaire would certainly, if the chance offered, do Rivière any ill, even to mortal injury; and now, as she walked cautiously along the street, she bitterly regretted the estrangement, and would have given years of her life to have been open with her husband, and consulted with him how to set danger at defiance.

But had he not shut her out fast from his confidence—cheated her, tricked her? Yes, and she had been angry and bitter, and had determined that she would give him secrecy for secrecy. But that was all past now. There was danger abroad, she was sure, and, let him deceive her as he would, her place was at his side.

Perhaps there was no reason for her great

anxiety this night; but it was foolish of him, so late, to go with that stranger. Why could he not have found his own way?

She had been looking for him so impatiently, regretting all the long evening that she had not persuaded him to stay at home, and had been up and down hour after hour, wildly anxious. All the same, though, she had made little excursions into the neighbouring streets, to see if she could find out where he was staying; always returning at the end of a few minutes, lest he should have arrived in her absence. At last, as it grew late and she was watching, she had seen him come, had seen him stopped by the stranger, had hurried down, and was now following him at a distance, with the determination of joining him as soon as he was alone, and of then telling him all her doubts and fears. There should be no more separation, no reticence on her side; she would tell him how Lemaire dogged her steps, and trust to him to save her from further molestation.

Yes, she would forgive him, and try to win him back by gentle love. She would not upbraid him with a word, or hint at her suspicion of his visits to Grosvenor-square, and all would yet be well.

That was strange!

A shiver passed through Marie Rivière's frame, as, after passing through street after street, always keeping her husband in sight, she first doubted, then made sure that three men were watching him—two being close upon his track.

She tried to throw off the suspicion. If she waited till they had gone a little farther, she felt sure that she would see them turn some other way.

She waited; and then grew hot and cold by turns, for they followed still. There was one, too, in front; and at the end of the next street her doubts resolved themselves into realities—Rivière was being watched.

Yes, there was no doubt of it now; and she

shortened the distance between them, the men being so intent upon their object that they did not notice her, or if they did paid no heed, taking her for some outcast of the night.

There would be something happen, then, as soon as Rivière had parted from this stranger, unless she was there ready to join him, when probably her presence would keep them at bay. He should go no more alone by night.

At one time she determined to speak to the policeman she met; but gave the project up the next moment, telling herself that there would be no necessity; for however nefarious the design, her presence would be sufficient to ward off danger.

She followed pretty closely, then, till the last street was reached; and then like a flash came the idea—suppose this stranger were one of the party?

The blood flew to her eyes, and her heart beat tumultuously. She would wait no longer, but join her husband at once. She hurried forward, trying hard to accelerate her pace, as by the light of the lamps she saw Rivière entering the open doorway, and the men close up as if driving him in.

Good Heaven! would she be too late? They would murder him before she could get there. Her feet seemed weighted, and everything was like some horrid nightmare, wherein she seemed to be held back; but in truth she had almost flown, and reached the open door to see a struggle going on, and in time to utter a piercing cry for help.

Four men were overpowering one whom they had taken by surprise, and a weak woman was sufficient in her devotion to put them to flight.

That one piercing cry was sufficient; they had not reckoned upon such an interruption, and with a wholesome dread of the legal executive of the country of their adoption, one and all fled, leaving Rivière half stunned as he staggered to his feet.

"Quick!" exclaimed Marie, leading him; and the next minute they were hurrying along the street, uninterrupted; for not a soul was to be seen.

One or two windows had been thrown up, and heads had been thrust curiously out, for their owners to gaze after the men, who ran down the street—two, the others having disappeared in the house; but as no further sound disturbed the night, and the cry had not reached the ears of the police, the windows were soon closed, and the fugitives reached their home in safety.

"Louis, we must not stay here longer—in this city," exclaimed Marie, trembling violently as she clung to her husband, now he was safe.

"You saved my life," he whispered, in a half-scared fashion. "I was trapped; but you were in time. It was yours, and you saved it."

"Yes, it is mine," she said, clinging to him, and gazing lovingly into his eyes. "You know, though, who has done this?"

"Yes," he said, hoarsely, as the veins stood up on his temples; "it was Lemaire."

"Yes," she said, shudderingly, "he is the evil genius of our lives."

CHAPTER X.

SIR RICHARD'S ANSWER.

THE next morning Marie Rivière told all of her own experience. How Lemaire had watched her day after day, and dogged her steps till she had dreaded to leave the house; and Rivière ground his teeth as he listened to the recital. It was in vain, though, that Marie besought him to stay within doors. He was not hurt in his last night's encounter, and this last intelligence, though it was no more than he had expected, was as fuel to a furnace already heated.

He promised to be back before dark, and to expose himself to no risks—that was the only concession he would make ; and then he hurried away, his blood boiling, and half furious now against Sir Richard Lawler.

Out in the busy streets, though, after walking for some time he grew a little calmer. He fell to thinking about Lady Lawler, and he regretted the collision for her sake. She had been so generous, so kind to Marie, in his distress.

" He does not comprehend our ways, this brutal Englishman," he muttered. "My faith, was he a pig-head, and had foolish thoughts ? She is good and kind ; but she is a great child, that wife of his. But," he continued, grimly, "she has a temper, and she will show it to him. Poor fool! Yes, he will send an apology, and I will forgive him. But the lessons? Ah, they are at an end."

This set him thinking of ways and means, and he strode on very fast through the streets, thinking, thinking ever ; but no good idea came.

"It is a cursed place, this London!" he said, shaking his clenched fist at the door of a handsome mansion. "How little, how very little would suffice to keep us, and yet we shall soon be ready to starve; anyhow, it is better than prison."

At length, tired out, he returned just as it was dark, to find Marie, pale and anxious, at the open window, eagerly watching for his coming.

A day passed—two days—three days. What should they do? Return to France? That was imprisonment for life. Stay where they were? That seemed to betoken starvation. Rivière walked up and down the room like a caged tiger.

Knock—no, bang!—at the door.

Rivière, with his soul panting within him, rushed to open it. Was it news? Was it an apology from Sir Richard Lawler?

The grubby face of a very small girl appeared, with tears wet on her cheeks, which she was polishing with the corner of a black-leady apron.

" If you plee, sir—"

" Oui, yes—speak, my child."

"Which I didn't want to come and say it, sir, but missus—"

" Yes, you have brought a letter."

" No, sir; and she says if you don't—" the child stopped—"don't leave off stamping, out you go."

The girl half shrieked the last words, in her dread of Rivière, who seemed, to use her own expression, about to fly at her; and half the sentence was uttered as she was hurriedly descending the stairs, to where her mistress was waiting in ambush ready to administer a cuff as the girl hurried by, with the result that there was a smothered cry, a slip, the bumping of some very badly encased bones upon the stairs, followed by a snivelling noise and a series of sobs from the mat.

"You hussey!" exclaimed a vinegary voice,

aloud, and it was meant for the girl, who had dared to fall; but it also ascended to Rivière, who closed his door softly, saying—

"Qu'est ce que c'est hussey?" And then he walked softly up and down the room, muttering to himself—"Madame is a little indisposed."

In fact he was thinking a good deal of the rent—a miserable minor matter that would intrude itself painfully, and clash with his stern notions of honour and a meeting with Sir Richard Lawler.

"It was very strange," he said; and then he grew elate, for an impatient knock resounded through the house, and, yes—no—yes—ah, yes, that was his name—a cry upon the stairs—

"Mister Rivvyer."

It was his landlady, and she had indeed a letter, which he took with eager eyes and carried to the window.

Yes! It was Sir Richard Lawler's hand, and addressed to the café, whence it had been sent to him; but Marie would see it! How awkward! How foolish of him not to call to-day and see if it had come! But he must open it, and he did, trying to tear open the great envelope with nonchalance, so as to leave the broad seal of the Lawlers untouched.

"Is it good news, Louis?" whispered a voice at his side. "Let there be no more secrets, my husband."

The envelope dropped from Rivière's hand. He stood, pale and panting; then without heeding his trembling wife, he placed the unread letter between his teeth, and tore and tore at it, dragging it away as he spat the fragments furiously about the room, until the missive was a mere litter of scraps.

"But he shall meet me!" he hissed, grinding his teeth. "Marie, it is too much."

"What is it?" she whispered, soothingly. "You did not read the letter."

"Read it? No, not now. My faith, no! But I did write it, write it to him; and the coward sends it to me back, marked across with his pen."

Marie was silent; she waited for his confidence, which did not come.

"Only another insult," he said, laughing, with a strange calm coming over him. "Our life grows eventful, dear one. But wait—wait—our time will come."

CHAPTER XI.

FOR HER SAKE.

DAYS passed, and still no confidence on the side of Rivière.

"She would be frightened," he reasoned with himself. "How can I tell her that I shall fight with him? It would drive her mad. Is it not enough that she knows of Lemaire, and the way he dogs us?"

But that danger seemed to be at an end. Rivière went in and out, at first cautiously, then with more daring; and at last he grew careless, in spite of Marie's prayers that he would be prudent.

"Bah!" he said. "The police will take

care of me, and I shall not be trapped again."

He went out to the cafés by night, and obtained a little teaching in the neighbourhood, just sufficient to enable him to keep body and soul together. He picked up friends, too—compatriots who frequented the various places of resort—and they were sociable to a degree, but they seemed as poor as himself.

By degrees, the bitter rage against Sir Richard Lawler seemed to fade away—not that he would not have gladly gone out to meet him; but privation and misery blunted his fine notions of honour, and he had to fight hard for a living.

Downward, always downward, seemed to be Louis Rivière's course, in spite of every effort; and now, after many months' sojourn in England, he found himself, with his wife in a state that needed his utmost care and attention, verging upon the borders of starvation. Lack of introduction had been his great difficulty, and those who could have introduced him were now his enemies.

"This must come to an end soon," Rivière said, bitterly, one morning, as he sat in their bare room. "I cannot suffer much more."

There was no reply from his pallid wife beyond that which came from her eyes.

What thoughts passed through the exile's breast need not be recorded here; they were interrupted by the sound of the landlady's voice—harsh, stringent, and defiant.

"Munseer Rivyer—Munseer Rivyer."

Rivière started trembling from his rickety chair, for this woman was an enemy he dreaded : he owed her weeks of rent.

"Do not let her come in, Louis, I cannot bear it," moaned his wife.

"No, mon enfant, she shall not come," exclaimed Rivière; and he ran to the door and held it fast.

"Munseer Rivyer!" came the voice again, "here's a letter."

"A letter!" exclaimed the exile, excitedly. "Mon Dieu! who would write to me?"

He took the letter, closed the door hastily, and hastened to the window; but a mist seemed to swim before his eyes, and his hand trembled so that he could not open it.

"It is some fresh trouble, Marie," he exclaimed to his wife, who was eagerly watching his every movement. "I cannot read it."

"Give it to me," she exclaimed, hoarsely.

He passed the letter, and with eager fingers she opened it, and read in French—

"DEAR COMPATRIOT—There are lessons to be given at the house of Lord Lynedale. I come to learn it this instant, and I think of thee. You must be—forgive me that I say it—welldressed, and ready with a good recommendation from some English family. You will rejoice to hear that I am gaining ground.—Yours,

"ADOLPHE MERCIER."

"And who is Adolphe Mercier?" asked Marie. "Pray beware."

"Only a poor compatriot that I have met at the café hard by," said Rivière, with brightening eyes, till he glanced down at himself. "But I am in rags, and I have no recommendation. Why did he show us this bright picture, when we cannot possess it?"

"Why—why," said Marie, hesitating—"why not ask those people to be your friends?"

"What people?" said Rivière, wonderingly.

"Those people who received us when we came."

"The Lawlers? Impossible!"

"No, Louis, it is not impossible," said Marie, clutching his hand in hers. "Ask them, and they will help you. I know what you think, and I own it all: I was foolish and weak, and I misjudged you. I know now that it was blind folly; but then that woman frightened me. I feared that she would rob me of all that was dear to me — your love. I ought to have known better; but you will forgive me."

The next moment he held her weeping to his breast.

"You will go—no, write and ask them, then, to help you in this our time of trouble."

"No, no, Marie, I cannot."

"Cannot? Oh, Louis, think of me!"

"Do not drive me mad, Marie. I do think of you night and day, but I cannot do that."

"Why not? You must not be proud now, Louis. Think, we are little more than beggars."

"Do you suppose I do not see that? But do not ask me, Marie."

"But I must, Louis. For your own sake—for my sake, pray, pray do this."

He hesitated for a few minutes, and then threw up his hands in despair.

"I cannot do it," he said.

No more passed then; but during the afternoon, Marie urged him again and again, telling him once more of her folly, and how she blamed herself for her jealousy, which had stood in the way of their advancement.

"But I will never be jealous of you again, Louis. And now you will write?"

"I cannot, Marie," he exclaimed; "you don't know all."

"But, indeed I do," she exclaimed.

And she urged him still, hour after hour, begging him at last with tears; until, feeling that the urgency must force him to forget all his own scruples, and sincerely regretting that he had acted towards his wife clandestinely in his visits to Grosvenor-square, but telling himself that it was impossible that he could enlighten her now, he sat down and wrote a few lines to Sir Richard Lawler, telling him in a quiet, gentle-manly way, that he looked upon the blows he had received as the result of a misconception— telling the baronet that he had wronged him cruelly; and ending by begging for assistance to enable him to seek and obtain the engagement his friend had intimated to him to be at liberty. He carefully abstained from mentioning Lady Lawler's name; and trusting to the Englishman's generosity, now that he had humbled himself, Rivière posted the letter, and felt almost light-hearted with hope and the victory he had gained over himself.

"It is for thy sake, Marie," he said.

"Yes," she whispered, lovingly; "and it will prosper. There will be an end to these dark clouds now, so let us be hopeful."

Rivière went out soon after. During his absence from home a few qualms of conscience again troubled him that he had not been open with his wife; but he waived them now, telling himself that the Lawlers would be friendly enough to help him, but there could be no more intimacy. It would be better that he should only avail himself of the introduction and a little monetary aid. He could pay that back soon. He saw himself, with all the Frenchman's sanguine temperament, already on the high road to fortune.

"Fate has done her worst for us now," he said. "We shall henceforth have sunshine."

He returned that night light-hearted and happy; for, let alone the hopefulness, he was glad that he had gained such a victory over self; and now he could have taken Sir Richard Lawler by the hand, and treated the past as something that had never been.

Poor Rivière! how different would have been his feelings could he have looked into the future as easily as he had read the bygone. He could not tell, though, that Sir Richard Lawler had received and replied to the letter. He could not tell that there had been bitterness for months between the baronet and his lady—the latter feeling that she was aggrieved by her husband's suspicions; and though before society the semblance of affectionate relations was kept up, and the servants only knew that there was a coolness between them, Lady Lawler declared that she would never forgive her husband until he had apologized to Rivière.

At first Sir Richard had treated this with contempt, laughingly telling himself that before long her ladyship would be glad to sue for pardon, he not having the slightest intention of carrying his anger and suspicion into the Divorce Court. He was disappointed, though; and surprised to find that his wife could be as obstinate as himself, quietly giving up society to a great extent, and settling down to the company of her child, of whom she was passionately fond; although Jane declared to her lover, Abram Higgs, that "she never see such fondness, never wanting to see the boy but twice a day, or three times at the most. If she ever had children—"

Here modesty taught Jane that she had gone farther than she meant, and she ended her discourse with a few sharp nods of the head.

Rivière woke light-hearted and happy; his sanguine imagination telling him that this was to be a bright and happy day for them both. Marie took her tone from him, and they ate their frugal breakfast with enjoyment, Rivière going out soon after to give a lesson—one of thirteen he was to impart for half a guinea.

"I shall be back by one," he said, "and then I shall stay at home and await the answer; though I do not expect it before evening. These aristocrats are very slow with the pen."

He nodded and departed—staying, however, a few moments to speak on the staircase to his waylaying landlady, whom he told hopefully that he should soon be able to pay now, and then hurried away to give his lesson.

Here, however, there was a shock for him, and which upon another occasion would have troubled him sorely ; this day he viewed the cross lightly, though he had but two pupils, and this was one.

It was but a repetition of that which he had learned again and again : a pupil who was the most eager to begin was the soonest tired of the tedious humdrum of the French regular and irregular verbs.

The lesson finished, Rivière walked cheerfully

back towards Soho, troubling himself but little that he was to give no more at the same place. His future wore a rosier aspect, and upon reaching the square it troubled him still less that he saw a man he took to be Lemaire hurriedly crossing the road.

"I have seen things in a bilious aspect," muttered Rivière, smiling; "and no wonder, when all looked so gloomy. Now for the letter."

He leaped lightly up a couple of steps at a time, and paused for a few moments, breathless, upon the landing before entering his room. He could not have said why, had he been asked, but something seemed to restrain him; the bright look-out of the future looked more dim, and an undefined sense of something wrong seemed to attack him and warn him back.

Was anything wrong with Marie? Pish! he was unstrung; and seizing the handle, he entered hastily, to confront his wife, standing, pale and set of teeth, her eyes seeming to flash as

she took a step forward to meet him, holding
out at arm's length a letter.

"Here!" she exclaimed, "see how cruel they
are, though we starve!"

Rivière snatched from her hand the open
letter, to read as follows :—

"I have had your letter, which is only
equalled in insolence by its cool villainy. You
ask me to give you money, and a recommendation into a noble family. What for? To in-
sinuate yourself into the favour of the lady of
the house, to wreck the happiness of another
home? Do you think I have forgotten the
scene that day when I returned to chastise your
insolence, after you had for weeks come to and
fro, generally unknown to me? I need say no
more; only that my servants have orders, in
case you should show yourself at my house, to
hand you over instantly to the police.

"RICHARD LAWLER."

For a few minutes Rivière stood as if stunned,

apparently unable to comprehend the gist of that which he read. He turned the letter in his hands, and gazed from it to his angry wife, who seemed to tower above him in her fierce passion; then he re-read the letter, with fury now beginning to flash from his own eyes, till a sound caught his ear which made him start and look around the room to find that he was alone, for Marie had run into her chamber, locking the door behind her, and now he could hear her raging, hysterical sobs where he stood.

The next moment he was shaking the chamber door furiously.

"Here, open this! Marie, Marie!" he said, angrily; but there was no response. He shook the door again and again, but it would not give way, neither could he elicit any reply.

He stood for an instant then, crushing the note in both hands before setting his teeth fast, and serving it as he had done the other, tearing it bit by bit into fragments to scatter upon the floor. A minute after, he made another ineffectual attempt to open the bed-room door, and then seized his hat and rushed from the house.

As the door closed, pale and agitated, her eyes swollen with weeping, Madame Rivière entered the room, listened for a moment to the descending hurried steps, and then posted herself, mournful and heartbroken, at the window, to see her husband tearing across the street. The next moment, however, he was lost to her sight.

CHAPTER XII.

AN UNFRIENDLY CALL.

N leaving home, there was a furious rage brewing in Rivière's heart as he hurried along by-street after by-street, avoiding mechanically the great artery bearing the name of Oxford, till he turned into Grosvenor - square, where he paused for a few moments, to gather breath and collect his thoughts, which were scattered by the furious tempest of passion raging within

him. Plans he had none: his only purpose was
to confront Lawler, take him by the throat and
half strangle him, and then to lash him till he
consented to give him the satisfaction of a gentleman. For what had he done?—what had he not
done? Had he not by his letter destroyed all
hope, when there was a prospect of a better
future? Had he not by his base accusations
almost overturned the reason of Marie, and made
her believe her husband to be a libertine and
scoundrel? The recollection of the old insult
came up once more, stronger than ever, to fan
Rivière's rage, as he hurried along one side of
the square, and reached the house just as a child,
whom he recognized as Lady Lawler's, was led
by the nurse into the house.

He paused for a few moments as the sight of
the little one recalled the face of the mother;
and for an instant he shrank from his purpose.
She was a good, kind-hearted woman: it would
trouble her, this visit of his.

What of his own wife, then—had she been

spared?—had she not been driven almost frantic by the treatment he had received?

He waited no longer, but thundered at the door, which was thrown open by one of the colossi in livery, another and Mr. Sellars the butler standing close behind, it being near the time when callers might be expected.

"I wish to see Sir Richard Lawler," exclaimed Rivière, and he stepped forward as if to enter; but the footman was immediately supported by his fellow, the two filling up the doorway.

"Sir Richard aint at home," said one of them insolently.

"When will he be at home?" asked Rivière, sharply.

"Don't know. Not for a week—p'r'haps not for a month."

"Not for a month?" said Rivière, incredulously.

"No; and if you've got anything to sell, we don't want any, do we, sir?" continued the man, turning with a leering grin to the butler, who now came closer.

"No, we don't want any," said the butler, puffing out his cheeks, and looking as dignified as his inane countenance would allow.

Rivière glanced sharply from one to the other, biting his lip to keep back his rage; and then he pressed forward to obtain entrance.

"It is a lie," he said, slowly. "You are paid to cheat me. He will be home soon, and I will wait till he comes."

"Now, what's the good of your being obstinit, Mr. Rivvyer?" said the butler, persuasively "Don't we tell you Sir Richard aint at home?"

As he spoke, he added the weight of his person to that of the footman and under-butler, completely blocking up the door.

"You tell me lies!" hissed Rivière, with all a Frenchman's excited gesticulation. "I don't believe you. I say he is at home. You insult me, too, with your 'don't want any.' I can see, my friend, into the milestone. You do not deceive me. I know you are told to say not at home. But I see through it all, and if he is away I will wait hours—days, till he does come. I *will* see him."

"But don't I tell you you can't see him?" said the butler, angrily.

"Stand away, canaille!" hissed Rivière, making a dash forward.

Then, there was a scuffle which lasted a few moments, a certain amount of hair powder was shed, and the stronger got the better of the weaker; but, all the same, Rivière in his fierce anger nearly gained an entrance.

"Shut the door, James, can't you?" puffed Mr. Sellars. "D'yer want him to get in? Bang it, if he don't get out of the way. I don't care if his hands is in—a-coming and tearing off a man's buttons in this way! Why don't you shut the door?"

"Well, how can I when he's got his foot stuck in it like this here?" grumbled James. "Let go, will you! Here, give a shove some on you."

Bang!

There had been a sharp tussle just at the last, a swaying to and fro, and then Rivière was suddenly sent back far enough on the steps for the door to be closed, with a report like thunder to go echoing through the house, while he was left raging and fuming outside.

He stood for a few moments irresolute, and then walked along all four sides of the square to cool himself, and overcome the rage and mortification which nearly drove him mad. He felt that everybody was watching, that every man he met knew his history, and had seen his troubles from beginning to end.

Once round the square, and he was angry as ever. He would see Sir Richard, and force him to meet him—to give him satisfaction. He would have forgiven him before; he had forgiven him. Had he not gone to him, as it were, hat in hand, as if saying—"Let the bygone be a bygone—let it be forgotten, only befriend me now." And what had been the result? He had insulted him more than ever, and driven his wife half mad with suspicion that the false charges made in the letter were true.

He would have revenge!

He made this last declaration aloud, and with a great number of r's, greatly to the alarm of a nervous old lady—an antiquated cook—who was standing with her hand upon the area bell of a house on the opposite side of the square.

But Rivière had passed on the next moment, and was hurrying towards Sir Richard Lawler's, determined to get an entrance by some means.

He walked past, though, two or three times, so as to collect himself; for he was conscious of a feeling of dizziness and confusion of intellect, when he knew that he required all his nerve and determination to overcome the opposition which he must encounter.

At last he walked sharply up the steps, and thundered at the door, standing back the next moment for a rush.

If he had stood close up, he might have gained his point; but as it was, he was in full view, and one of the servants made a careful observation from one of the side windows, afterwards declining to open the door.

Rivière bit his lips with anger; for he caught a glimpse of the powdered head.

He repeated the knock, and waited.

No answer.

He knocked again.

No answer.

Seizing the knocker, he thundered at it again till there was the sound of a rattling chain being put up, the catch was drawn back, and the door opened.

He immediately threw himself against it; but to his chagrin it only gave way for a few inches, and jarred against the chain, while his face was close up to that of Mr. Sellars, who was speaking to him through the slit.

"Now, just look here, Mr. Rivvyer, this sort of thing may do in France, but it won't do here; so take my advice and go. My orders from Sir Richard was that if you come to the house and made any bother, I was to send for the police. Now, air you going away quietly, or am I to send for the police?"

"I will see your master," said Rivière, wrathfully.

"But you can't; and I tell you what it is, sir, if you don't go, I ra'ally will send for the police; for I aint going to have my door knocked about like that, so I tell you."

"Tell your master that he is a cur — a coward—a scoundrel—a poltroon!" exclaimed Rivière, livid now with fury, and shaking his fist impotently at the door; till, seeing that a crowd was fast collecting, he strode away, trying to calm the passion that surged in his breast.

For some distance he was followed by a straggling tail of boys, who watched him narrowly for the length of quite a couple of streets, and then began to drop off on finding that he had ceased to gesticulate.

CHAPTER XIII.

A FRACAS.

IT was growing dark, and the lamps were beginning to twinkle along the far-reaching streets, till they shone in the distant perspective like rows of golden beads, ever approaching nearer and nearer. Carriages were passing here and there in the better-class streets, each bearing its freight of lightly clad inmates—the proportion being one lady taking up three-quarters of a vehicle, the gentleman the other fourth. Every here and there, too, in the street and square, the front doors of mansions were open, and the staff of servants calmly surveying fashionable life from the steps, indicating to all passers-by that "our people" were out to dinner.

As Rivière passed group after group of these well-fed idlers, he glanced at them half enviously as he saw the complete absence of care on their smooth, sleek visages. But his rage was still too hot within him to take much heed, and he passed on till he once more reached Sir Richard's house in the square.

There was a chariot at the door now, with a pair of horses pawing impatiently at the road. What did it mean?

He paused to think for a few moments, then the answer came: they were going out to dinner.

It was most unfortunate, he told himself: he could not strike the husband in the presence of the wife. He would wait, though, he thought—it might be Sir Richard going alone; and if so, he was certain of such an interview as would enforce a meeting.

"Let me strike him on the cheek before

his servants, and he cannot refuse to meet me."

Half an hour did he wait, with the obstinate pertinacity of a dog; and then, at last, a footman stepped out bearing a roll of horsehair carpet, which was rolled down from the steps, across the pavement to the carriage door. A minute later, Lady Lawler, looking extremely handsome in her full evening dress, made her appearance, and walked quickly down to the carriage; then the steps were rattled up, the door closed; the footman gave his orders to the coachman, and sprang up behind; when, as the carriage was moving off and Lady Lawler in the act of drawing up the window, she caught sight of Rivière's pale, angry face.

He did not hear it, but she uttered a faint cry, and stretched out one hand to him, as with the other she sought the check-string.

Rivière was, for the moment, about to spring forward; but there seemed to interpose itself between them the pale, despairing face of his wife ; and then he recalled the treatment he had received from Sir Richard and his servants. The indecision was gone in an instant, and he shrank hastily back.

His movement was not unseen : Lady Lawler saw the action, and the carriage rolled on unchecked, with her ladyship bound for a dinner party—Sir Richard dining that evening at his club.

It might have been better for all had the carriage been stopped, and Lady Lawler said a few friendly words to the excitable little Frenchman ; for she would probably have checked the torrent of rage waiting to be poured in fury upon her husband. But it was not to be ; and half an hour after, Lady Lawler had all but forgotten the incident.

Rivière had hardly eaten or drunk that day ; but still he stayed on, pacing about, never losing sight of the house, only refreshing himself from time to time with a pinch of tobacco rolled deftly up between his lithe fingers into a cigarette. Hour after hour passed, but no Sir Richard. There had been plenty of false alarms, carriages and cabs driving up; but no Sir Richard.

He had seen the chariot return and enter a mews close by; and a couple of hours later he saw it reissue, and drive off—to return an hour farther on, with Lady Lawler inside.

For a few seconds he felt disposed to run up and hand her out, for she was still alone; but something seemed to check him. He felt that he was not fit company for a refined woman; for he was half mad. But as he stood in the shelter of a neighbouring doorway, he saw the light flash from her jewels as she half paused on the carriage step and glanced in each direction, as though to see if he were there.

He shrank back into the shadow, and in another few seconds she had passed from sight, the long roll of carpet was drawn in, and where a moment before there had been a long, well-defined flood of light, lay blackness, showing that the hall door had been suddenly closed. Almost at the same instant the carriage rattled by, and the great square was sombre and deserted once more.

It was a weary task; but Rivière did not seem to feel it. Sir Richard was out somewhere; and he paced up and down, up and down, with untiring patience—his lips pale as his cheek, but his eyes seeming to blaze, as he turned again and again, now on the pavement, now in the road, from whence he could look up and watch the windows.

He knew the internal economy of the house pretty well, and he noted as he looked up that there was a light in the nursery, another in the drawing-room—that was all; and he argued that Lady Lawler was awaiting the coming of her husband, otherwise she would have retired to rest, and he should have also seen a light in Sir Richard's dressing-room.

He was not away; he was sure of that. The

servants had been told to lie to him, and deny that their master was at home; and he — he, Louis Rivière, would stay till he dropped; but he would smite him on the cheek, and tell him he was a liar and a coward.

Twelve had struck, and the carriages which rumbled through the streets were fewer and farther between. A policeman had turned upon him his bull's-eye, and passed out of sight; and still no Sir Richard. It must have been close upon one when, as if electrified, Rivière started from where he had been leaning against the iron railings of the square garden, and threw away his cigarette; for there came now the sharp rattle of a Hansom cab.

He was on the kerb before it could reach the door; for instinct seemed to have told him his enemy was at hand. The blood danced in his veins, as the cab drew up sharply. Then a tall figure sprang lightly out, handed half-a-crown to the driver, and was in the act of turning, when a hand was placed upon his throat, and he stood face to face with Rivière.

"You have insulted me!" the latter ground out between his teeth.

"Stand back, you scoundrel!" exclaimed Sir Richard, whose flushed face betokened that he had been drinking heavily, and he tried to force his way past his assailant. But, active as a cat, Rivière fixed his other hand in the baronet's necktie; and though he was swung back by the stronger man, managed to hold on tenaciously.

"Look here!" exclaimed Rivière, panting, "dog of an Englishman that you are! You have insulted me. Will you give me the satisfaction of a gentleman?"

Sir Richard's reply was a heavy blow across his assailant's face with his umbrella.

"Another blow!" hissed Rivière, savagely. "You force me to fight like you canaille of English—like a groom or brute beast!"

And loosening one hand, he struck Sir Richard two or three smart blows in the face in return.

Here the struggle was interrupted by the cab-man, who sprang off his perch just as the hall door was flung open, to bathe the whole scene with light; and the sleepy footman, after staring aghast for a moment or two, hurried out to his master's assistance.

Even now a crowd was collecting—one of those heterogeneous assemblies which, no matter what the hour of the day or night, seem suddenly to spring up from nowhere, no one knows how; and opinions were passing pretty freely upon what the spectators called the row.

Last of all, and very leisurely, just as the voices were loudest and most excitable, came a police-man, not in the slightest degree out of breath, and in time to hear Rivière shriek rather than say—

"Will you give me the satisfaction now, or must I tear you like a dog? Will you meet me?"

"No, you scoundrel—no!" cried Sir Richard, hoarsely, who, thoroughly roused, was now able to hold his weaker antagonist easily at bay.

"Fair play!" cried the crowd.

"Yes, let 'em have fair play!" said a ragged-looking rough, shouldering off the footman, while a couple more held back the cabman from interfering.

"Here, policeman!" exclaimed Sir Richard, who was the first to see the new-comer, "I give this fellow into custody. He has assaulted me —look here!"

The turned-on bull's-eye had already shown the constable the bleeding face of the baronet, and he had also taken in the scene at a glance— making out that one of the contending parties was dressed as a gentleman, and that the other was shabby in the extreme.

"Here, you make yourself scarce," said the policeman to the big rough; "and you button up your coat, sir, unless you want to lose that there chain," he continued, turning to Sir Richard, whose light paletot had been torn open from top to bottom. "Now, then—assault, is it? Any witnesses?"

"Yes, plenty," exclaimed Sir Richard, still panting with his exertions; for Rivière was writhing fiercely in his grasp. "Here's the cabman who brought me from the club. My servant, too, he saw part of it. Hold this man, will you? There, that is my card. This is my house. I am Sir Richard Lawler."

"Sir Richard's got it 'ot, aint he?" sniggered one of the crowd, and there was a laugh.

"Mounseer aint got nothing to brag about," said another.

Then there was silence as all pressed forward to listen to the conversation.

"All right, sir," said the policeman; "you'll have to appear. P'r'aps you'll come on in your cab, and enter the charge?"

"Stop!" exclaimed Rivière, twisting his arm loose from the constable's clutch; "he has assaulted me—he has insulted me—he dares not give me in charge!"

And he strove once more to get near Sir Richard.

"Come, none o' that, you know!" exclaimed the policeman, getting a tighter hold, and giving his prisoner an official shake. "You'd better come on quietly."

"Yah! Let the poor man go!" cried two or three in the crowd, now ready to help what they considered the poor and oppressed against the rich.

"I will not go—I protest," exclaimed Rivière. "Sir Richard, this is a greater act of cowardice than ever."

And he shivered at the officer's touch; for it brought up France—his trial and imprisonment.

"None o' that, I tell you!" exclaimed the policeman, trying to make a· move; but the crowd held firm, and there was an ominous buzz—the words, "Let the poor man go," being heard again, while Sir Richard was more than once roughly hustled, and his hat knocked off; for seeing that he wore a valuable watch and chain, several members of the crowd had grown wonderfully chivalrous on behalf of the suffering foreigner. Perhaps something more stirring would have taken place—resulting, possibly, in a rescue—had not another policeman come slowly up to fortify his brother of the staff, the couple proceeding to lead off their prisoner.

There was also another diversion to take the attention of the crowd; for a lady suddenly appeared in full dress at the hall door, and ran down to where Sir Richard stood wiping his face, and about to leap into his cab; for the driver had once more resumed his place, and had whispered to him to jump in, if he didn't want to have his pockets picked.

"Oh, Richard, what is this?"

"What!—you here?" he replied, angrily. "Your work, if you must know," he added, in a low voice. "Go in at once, and let's have no more scandal."

"Is that Monsieur Rivière?" she exclaimed, pointing towards the retreating figure with the police. "I saw him to-night. Oh, Richard," she whispered, "you have never been so base—"

"So base as to give the ruffian into custody for assaulting me? Yes, ma'am, I have. Wait, cabby," he said, aloud. And then, catching Lady Lawler by the arm, he hurried her through the thinning crowd to the door, and stayed till it was closed.

The next minute Sir Richard's cab was rattling along towards the police-station; Lady Lawler was crying hysterically in the drawing-room; and the footman was busy relating the incidents of the fracas to the sleepy under-butler in the servants' hall.

"And where's Sir Richard, then?" said the under-butler.

"Gone to the police station to see the little Frenchman locked up."

"And serve him right!"

CHAPTER XIV.

A NIGHT IN A CELL.

IT would perhaps be hardly fair to blame policemen for their peculiarities; for many of their failings are, we forget, not peculiar to the policeman, but to man in general. All the same, if something happens — if they carry out a task in a way we should hardly have noticed from an ordinary mortal, we come down heavily upon the constable—morally, not physically—and say, "That's your police, all over."

This is called forth from the fact that a great deal of the justice meted out in our police-stations—not courts—by the inspector on duty is strongly tinged by faith in dress as allied to position in society. If a prisoner be rough and ill-clad, and the prosecutor arrayed in nineteenth century purple and fine linen — which is, of course, black cloth—your policeman will, of a certainty, say, "You sir" to the former, and "Sir" to the latter; and be disposed to look upon his as the words of truth and wisdom, while he will regard the rough and ill-clad prisoner as the greatest liar under the sun.

It was a case in point upon the arrival at the station, poor Rivière having had rather an unpleasant time of it, inasmuch as he had been most desirous, on the way, of entering into explanations, and had made stoppages for expostulation—all of which had been looked upon as so many feeble attempts to escape, or enlist the sympathies of the crowd in his favour; and judging from actual facts, as well as from tradition, there is no one upon whom your police-constable would sooner "come down hard" than upon him who invites help from the spectators.

Rivière, then, reached the police-station in a condition that was far from likely to obtain sympathy from that Rhadamanthus of the time, the inspector in charge; for the prisoner's face was swollen and marked with blood, his shabby garments were pulled all awry, and he was in a state of voluble excitement when placed in the little iron dock, which almost precluded any one from speaking but himself.

"It was a case of insult," he cried. "Sir Richard—"

"Will you hold your tongue?" cried the inspector. "Let the gentleman make his charge."

"But—"

"Give over with you," said the policeman who had brought him in.

Then Sir Richard began to make his statement. ·

"I tell you," said Rivière, "it was—"

"Come, none o' that, now," was the next admonition; and Rivière was again silent, while Sir Richard advanced enough for the inspector to enter the charge—more than he had done half an hour before, when two voluble women, tattered and torn by warfare, had been before him, and he had told them both to "be off home, and not quarrel any more."

And now Rivière tried to appeal once more; but there was not much chance of his being heard at that late hour of the night. And here were the facts: a baronet, residing in Grosvenor-square, gave a very shabby-looking foreigner, who said he had no address, into custody on a charge of assault, witnessed by the cabman who brought the baronet from his club.

Result : Sir Richard Lawler, very bitter and angry, walked back to his cab; while Louis Rivière, choking with indignation, was hurried off to a cell, where he sat in the dark, meditating revenge.

Certainly, one policeman did give him a hint—

"Tell the inspector your address, and send for some friends to bail you out."

But what friends had he? Who would be his securities? And besides, just then his mind was in too great a state of chaos for it to hold anything more than rage and hatred against Sir Richard Lawler.

It was hard work, though, to sit in that close cell, with a policeman coming from time to time to flash a light over him through the little grating in the door, and make sure that he was neither in a fit, nor suspending himself, in a moment of mad fury, by his stockings or handkerchief.

But Rivière had no such thoughts; for now he was in trouble about Marie, and the old feelings of the French prison came over him, making him shudder again. Then he thought of her anxiety, in spite of the past day's anger. What would she think of his absence? Heaven, what a position! And all brought about by the brutal letter and insolence of Sir Richard.

It was a night to be remembered, as its small hours passed sluggishly by, the prisoner's eyes hardly closing. Now some human beast, furiously drunk, would be dragged in, howling, cursing, and blaspheming with twenty-demon power, forced into a cell roughly, and perhaps rather viciously, by the capturing constables ; and small wonder, when he had been striking out, right and left, till his arms were mastered, after which he had made up for the deprivation by kicking with all his might. Twice over this occurred, with the same result—that the prisoner immediately settled down into a drunken stupor, to be heard no more, save as the emitter of heavy, stertorous snores.

Perhaps Rivière would settle himself with his back in a corner, and begin, as he grew cooler, to think about his prospects of release in the morning; for he now began to feel sure that Sir Richard would never dare to face him in the court. Then, feeble with fasting and his previous day's exertions, his head would fall upon his chest, and for a few moments he would dose, but only to be roused again by the shriek of some gin-mad harridan, borne in upon a stretcher, and who, upon being relegated to the comparative freedom of a cell, began, immediately upon being left alone, to resent the solitude, and beat furiously at the door, making the place re-echo with her cries. This served to set others off; voices would be heard at gratings, asking if the police were murdering the "poor woman;" while others raved, roared, and cursed, till silenced by the gaoler rapping sharply at door after door—at times, too, threatening the more obstreperous of the inmates.

Rivière's cell, though, seemed to take up the largest share of his attention; and, not content with casting a light and peering through the bars, he would open the door and speak to his wild, haggard little prisoner, who raised his face and responded with a short, sharp shake of the head.

Rivière's longest sleep was not of more than a few minutes' duration, and from this he woke with a start, alarmed by louder cries than usual. There seemed to be a good deal of light, too ; and for an instant he felt ready to start up, panic-stricken ; for it seemed to him that there was a fire once more in his prison, and that his life was in peril.

"Let it come," he said, sadly, as he sank back in his place; "life is not worth much to me."

Morning at last—coming very slowly, and with weak, cold rays to the cells of the police-station. The noisy occupants had settled down, one by one, to sink, for the most part, into the stupor caused by drink; but there was no feeling of calm for Rivière. The cool air came softly through the little grating; but it did not take the fever from the cheek he laid against the wall, as he now stood longing for freedom.

For as he thought more and more of the position, it seemed the height of folly to imagine that Sir Richard would come forward. He would certainly be content with having ridded himself of his assailant, and condone the assault for the sake of avoiding the annoyance that must result from a public inquiry. And as to the magistrate, no doubt he would be sharply admonished by him, and then set at liberty.

CHAPTER XV.

FIVE POUNDS OR A MONTH.

THE hour for the hearing of his case seemed to Rivière as if it would never come. The morning was cold, dull, and depressing; and he needed not the sinking sense of hunger, the aching head, and bruised limbs to make him thoroughly wretched. How thought, too, would come, full of inventions of troubles that might never happen; especially as he heard cell door after door opened, and the rough, sharp voice of the police summoning the offenders, some of whom had to be shaken from their heavy, drunken sleep before they staggered out.

One hour—two hours! Would his case never be called?

He was busy, though, planning and determining what he would say in his defence; and if Sir Richard Lawler did appear, how he would shame him by telling in open court of the cowardice of his nature, and how he had refused to give the satisfaction of a gentleman.

"These islanders do not like duelling; but still they have their ideas of honour," he said to himself.

And then he once more applied his face to the grating, waiting till a policeman should come near enough to be addressed.

At last one came.

"How long will it be before I am called up?" Rivière inquired.

"Don't you fret yourself," was the response; "you'll be called up a deal sooner than you'll like, I'll lay."

Then the man passed on to another cell,

where he led out one of the noisy gin victims—
mad and uproarious the night before ; this
morning, limp, whining, and tearful, a bundle of
dirty rags more than a woman ; but which
addressed the policeman as " my dear," and
begged hard for " a drink o' water."

But the longest period of suspense comes to
an end at last, and in his excitable fashion
Rivière was ready to leap out upon his door
being opened, hurrying along by the side of the
officer to the court.

He had done what he could to make himself
presentable ; but a station cell is not well
furnished with toilet requisites, and he knew
that his appearance must militate terribly
against him, and he could not help asking
himself, bitterly, what there was to distinguish
him from the commonest offender who had
gone up before.

The buzzing of voices in the court interrupted
his thoughts; and before he could thoroughly
realize his position, he was standing in the dock,

before a host of faces, and listening to the voice of the clerk.

Would Sir Richard appear? That was the question which filled Rivière's mind, to the exclusion of court, magistrate, all else. A few moments would decide, for his name was called now in a loud voice.

A thrill of excitement ran through the prisoner's frame as he waited what seemed an interminable space of time for the response, which came at last, and he saw the baronet step quietly up into the box, with his face discoloured and a narrow strip of black sticking-plaister across one temple.

He was perfectly composed, and studiously refrained from looking in the direction of the man he accused, as he calmly stated his case.

Rivière bore this for awhile; but an assertion the baronet made was like the spark to a train of powder, and he began to expostulate in loud tones.

" It is not true, it is not true, Sir Richard."

"Silence, sir!" exclaimed the magistrate.

"But I cannot be silent when this man makes such statements," exclaimed Rivière.

"Hold your peace, and wait. You shall have an opportunity of defending yourself by and by.'

Rivière set his teeth hard, glanced at the prosecutor, and listened while Sir Richard went on, glibly enough, telling of how he was returning from his club, and had reached his own door, when he was set upon by the defendant.

"But why—why?" cried Rivière, excitedly. "Did you not refuse me the satisfaction of a gentleman?"

"I refuse to answer such questions," said Sir Richard, haughtily. "I keep to my statement that I was violently assaulted by the defendant."

"But you did strike me," cried Rivière.

"Of course," said Sir Richard, "in self-defence."

And then, Rivière being silenced, the baronet went on again, carefully suppressing all allusions as to past knowledge of the defendant, and all reasons for the attack.

Here Rivière would have once more dashed in with eager declarations, but he was again checked, threatened with punishment for contempt of court, and at last thoroughly silenced; to stand glaring angrily from one to the other of those present, as if he felt himself entirely surrounded by enemies.

Then the cabman was put in the box and sworn.

"John Judson" his name was, he said; "and this here gent—the big un, not the little un—come out of the Blue—"

"Out of the what?"

"Out of the Blue—the club, you know—and 'Drive me home,' he sez. 'Where's that, sir?' I sez, laughing; for the gent was a bit on, your worship."

"Confine yourself to the simple facts, my good fellow," said the magistrate.

"That is fax, your worship," said the man.

"Why, the gent don't go for to say as he warn't a bit on?"

"I'll admit that I was somewhat excited," said Sir Richard, from the body of the court.

"There is no occasion for you to speak, sir," exclaimed the magistrate, tetchily. "Really, this is most irregular. Go on, sir, at once."

"Well, your worship," continued the cabman, ' Drive me home,' he sez; and at last I got down and helped him to get his card-kis out, and read his number under a lamp, and drove him to Grosvenor-square."

"Go on," said the clerk, who was taking down the deposition.

"Yes, your worship; and I s'pose the ride pulled him together a bit, for he got out steady enough, when up comes the little chap—"

"If you mean the defendant, say so," interrupted the magistrate.

"Just so, your wor—I mean, sir—up comes the little defendant, and sez something, and then one hits t'other, and t'other hits back, and they was lugging one another awful for a bit, till I stopped 'em, and the pleece came—when it was all over," he added, in a low voice.

"And you will swear that the defendant assaulted the prosecutor?"

"Oh, theer warn't no doubt about that, your worship; he 'salted him, fast enough, and t'other 'salted him back—'ot! He took it out of 'im again pretty well."

"That will do—stand down."

The cabman stood down, and gave place to a very streety-looking individual, who swore boldly to the assault, and stated his conviction that the "little furrener" meant the gent's watch and chain.

"Canaille!" muttered Rivière, contemptuously.

Lastly came the policeman, who deposed to taking the charge, and finding the greatest difficulty in keeping the defendant at bay. He was about the bloodthirstiest man of his size the constable ever recollected to have met with; and was offering to fight the prosecutor with pistols or swords all the way to the station.

Rivière made his defence, which was cut short; and the magistrate delivered a speech in a very thick, unctuous tone of voice, and quite ignoring the fact that there were half a dozen solicitors and barristers impatiently awaiting the turn of their clients, who were still in the cells of the court. But the gentleman in question loved to hear his voice enunciating moral platitudes, and he made a point of telling Sir Richard that it was very evident that there was something disreputable at the bottom of this case; though it was not the business of the Court to probe that to the end. It was enough that it had been made out to the satisfaction of the bench that a violent assault had been committed, and for that assault it was his duty to punish the defendant—a man of dangerous passions—by fine or imprisonment. He must say, though, that it was—yes, he would use the word—disgraceful that an English gentleman, a baronet, could so far forget himself as to get into a state of intoxication, and be mixed up with such an affair.

It was only by an effort that Sir Richard, who was fuming and chafing under this exordium, continued to keep silence. He told himself, again and again, that if he had known what was to follow he would never have given Rivière into custody; for, in spite of his anger, he was pleased to find the chivalrous manner in which the little Frenchman avoided all reference to Lady Lawler. He became somewhat calmer, though, upon the magistrate's eloquence being turned on to the defendant, who was also severely admonished about the evils attendant upon the habit of allowing his angry passions to rise. In fact, at one time it seemed as if his worship was about to repeat, for the defendant's behoof, a few verses from the poems of the celebrated Dr. Watts; but he refrained, and went on preaching in prose, to Rivière's great disgust—

the latter folding his arms and gazing full at him, with a look of the most profound contempt pervading every feature, till the last words of the long-winded speech fell upon him like a thunderclap—

"Be fined fine pounds and costs, or a month's imprisonment, without hard labour."

"Five pounds!—a month!" gasped Rivière.

"Yes," said the magistrate; "and then, if you will take my advice, you will at once leave this country, and get back home, where pistols and swords may be more palatable to the people at large than they are here."

This was said jocularly, and his worship looked round for a smile, which was, of course, accorded to him, in company with a little murmuring.

This was, however, immediately suppressed, attention being taken up by the excited gestures of Rivière, who first fell back, and then started forward, clutching wildly at the dock.

"Five pounds!—a month!" he exclaimed;

"but this is not justice. I could not pay so much. You do favour that man, and oppress—"

"Silence!"

"I will be heard," he exclaimed, rendered almost frantic by his position. "You shall—"

"Are you prepared to pay?" asked a stern voice.

"No, no—I protest—I—"

There was a nod given, and two strong hands were laid upon the defendant's collar. For a moment he thought of resistance; but his good sense warned him of its futility, and he suffered himself to be led quietly away to a cell, the last words he heard upon leaving the court being a call for the next case.

CHAPTER XVI.

AN OFFER.

WHAT should he do—what should he do?
He was safe from the plotting of
Lemaire here, he told himself, grimly.
But was he? There was that poor, defence-
less woman, too. She must be protected; but
how?

Rivière would have paced his cell, but there
was not room; and he threw himself upon the
wooden board, and thought.

Five pounds or a month—five pounds or a
month; and he without the means of paying five
shillings. He had not a friend to whom he could
apply. But was there no appeal? No; there

could be no appeal in this case. It was open to him to pay the fine, and then he would be at liberty. But the money?

And the alternative—a month's imprisonment. He might have borne it, as he had borne imprisonment before, but for Marie, and the knowledge that she was pursued by that fiend. He must be free, or he should go mad; and as for that cur, that coward, that miserable wretch, Lawler, he would have a revenge upon him that should embitter his life to the very end.

Yes, he would be revenged on him; but how? How to get free? Five pounds—such a pitiful, paltry sum; and yet standing up like a huge rock before him to bar the way. While Marie— Heaven! what would she think? It would kill her if she knew. Better perhaps, though, that she should die than live on in such misery; only let her die with faith in him—her husband, to the last.

Yes, it was very bitter. His enemy, a coward, had triumphed because he was rich and respectable, and had money; while the poor refugee—

Would have revenge yet—would strike the coward in his tenderest part; and make him suffer, even as did the victim of his oppression now.

Then he calmed down, and sat and thought systematically as to what should be his course.

First, he decided that he must bear his fate like a man, merely sending to Marie to be on her guard; telling her, if he were allowed to write, that he was ever her own husband, that he was kept away by friends, and that she was to be cautious and wait patiently for his return.

She must never know, he argued; for she was a poor tender woman, and she would be horror-stricken if she comprehended one-half. She must never know, either, of his determination to be revenged on Sir Richard Lawler.

"Poor girl," he said, and a soft smile spread over his worn face—"she was angry then with her suspicions, but that would soon pass over;

and if I were there she would be ready to ask me to forgive her for her mad rage."

But the next minute maddening thoughts came upon him about how she would be left alone once more to the tender mercies of the world.

" She will be a match for all," he muttered. " Let them touch her if they dare!"

His eyes flashed in the dark, as he stood there in the dim obscurity of the cell, and gazed defiantly about him; till a crushing thought came, so bewildering, so maddening, that after throwing up his clenched hands above his head, he sank down with a groan upon the floor, and crouched there, sobbing and moaning like a beaten child.

" She will think I have forsaken her—that I have left her for Lady Lawler." She had believed him false when she had read that accursed letter; and now, as he did not return, even if he wrote, she would believe ill of him; for had he not deceived her before?

"But I will be a man," said Rivière, at last; and he sprang up once more. "She would go to Grosvenor-square if she thought that, and there she would learn the truth. Let her, perhaps it would be best."

And now the time began once more to flag heavily; and he sat thoughtful, and wondering whether this was to be his cell, or whether he would be removed, when a policeman came and opened the door.

"Let's see, your name's Rivvyer, aint it?"

"Yes."

"This here's a note for you."

"Ah, Marie! she has learned, then."

"Eh?"

"Who is it from?"

"Oh, from that there gent as you—"

"Take it back, take it back!" exclaimed Rivière; "I do not know him—I do not see him. He is a scoundrel. I will not have to do with him at all."

"There, don't be in a fuss," said the policeman,

kindly. "What a fiery little fellow you are. You're for all the world like a chap in a play Why don't you take it coolly? 'taint the first time you've been in prison, I'll bet."

Rivière started; he was staggered, and the man's words had more influence over him than he could have thought possible.

"Look here," continued the constable, "it's no use to kick against your luck. Here's this gent that you pitched into, disposed to come round and be friends; leastwise, it seemed so from the way he spoke about you."

Rivière looked from the note to the policeman, and back again.

"Did he give you that letter?"

"Yes, wrote it out there, in the inspector's office, and seemed quite cooled down like; so the best thing you can do is to cool down the same, and be friends."

"You do not know what you say," said Rivière, hoarsely; "but let me see — let me read the note. Perhaps," he added to himself, "he will apologize; or," his eyes flashed, "he knows that he is a coward, and will give me satisfaction."

He tore open the note, and, getting close to the door, read, in a great, sprawling hand, written in pencil—

"Give me your word of honour, as a French gentleman, that neither I nor my family shall see or hear from you again, and I will forgive your violence of last night, pay the fine and costs for you, and set you at liberty.—R. L."

Rivière stood motionless, with his eyes fixed on vacancy; and the paper he held between his fingers trembled like a wind-blown leaf: Marie and freedom beckoning to him on one side; a gaol, misery, and torturing suspense on the other.

Those were the two mental pictures upon which Louis Rivière gazed—now leaning towards the one, now drawn to the other.

It was a hard struggle, and well would it have been for all concerned had he been won over to peace and forgiveness. But no; the smart of the blows he had received was too fresh, and the injustice from which he fancied he had suffered still rankled too strongly in his breast. He wavered no longer. What!—give up his idea of revenge, submit tamely and like a cur to this purse-proud Englishman, who would not give him an honourable meeting? No, he would sooner die.

"Well, what's the answer?" said the policeman, who had been watching him curiously.

"That!" said Rivière, proudly, and as he spoke he tore the note in two, and placing the pieces together tore them again. "Give those pieces to Sir Richard Lawler, the English baronet and gentleman, and tell him that that is the poor refugee's answer. Tell him that I look upon him as a coward and a scoundrel, and tell him that a French gentleman, however poor, cannot stoop to an act that is mean."

The policeman uttered a low whistle, and the door was closed.

"Well," said Sir Richard, "what did he say?"

"Let out like a madman, sir, and called you all sorts of names. Said I was to give you this."

Sir Richard Lawler muttered an oath as he took the scraps of paper, crushed them in his hand, and thrust them into his pocket.

"He will be cooler when he has had a month in prison," he said to himself. "Cursed unfortunate! I wish I had never seen the miserable little beggar. What will Addy say?"

For another hour after the door closed Rivière was left to his bitter thoughts. Then the daylight once more flashed into his cell, and a couple of officials appeared.

Was he ready to pay the fine and costs?

No.

Then in half an hour he would have to go to the House of Correction.

Good.

The door closed once more.

"He's an old bird, that," said one to the other; "he's been in the cage before—don't mind it a bit."

"The little Frenchman's a-going to take it out, Dick," said the other to a friend in the court soon after.

Then the notice was given over to the clerk. The reporters obtained the scrap of news, feeding their note-books with it greedily; and at the end of the notices, in the morning papers, headed "Disgraceful Assault in High Life," appeared the words—

"The prisoner, not being provided with the necessary amount, was removed in the prison van."

CHAPTER XVII.

SYMPTOMS.

IT was a very observant policeman who was on duty in Grosvenor-square, and he took a great deal of notice of what went on at the different houses. He could have told you the names of all the inhabitants, and when they went out to dinner, and when they stayed at home; when they had company, and when they spent the evening at the Opera. The servants, too, came largely under his observation; and perhaps he knew more of the area business than he did of that appertaining to the front door. His name was Wilkins—P.C. Wilkins, and he had a grievance. Smith had been made a sergeant, and Tompkins had now been promoted to Smith's post, while Smith was a full-blown inspector. It was very bad, very; for he, P.C. Wilkins, was P.C. Wilkins still.

He was on day duty now, for a change, was P.C. Wilkins; and as he slowly walked by the house of Sir Richard Lawler, he beat his gloves together, and thought over the assault case, and wondered whether the baronet would tip him.

" He ought to," mused P.C. Wilkins. " Why that little Frenchman would have torn him like a tarrier if I hadn't come up. But there, what gratitude is there in this world? Here have I done more for our division than any man in the force, and what's my reward?—here am I only a P.C., and everybody else is made sergeants and inspectors."

Now, this was a slight exaggeration caused by

acidity of temperament. P.C. Wilkins was not
in a good temper. He had reckoned, after being
up as witness at the court on the Lawler-Rivière
case, upon getting an off evening; but a brother
constable had had his hat knocked off in a
public-house row, and an excited Irishman had
applied to his bare head a pewter quart pot with
more vigour than had been necessary—the result
being that the Irishman had gone to prison, and
the constable to bed; while P.C. Wilkins was on
the injured brother's beat.

"What's up there now?" muttered P.C. Wilkins. "That's another little Frenchman hang-
ing about there, smoking his bits of screwed-up
tobacco, or I'm a Dutchman. What's his little
game?"

P.C. Wilkins kept his eye on the stranger, and
passed him.

"Another little Frenchman it is," he muttered,
"and there's another assault case on. P.C.
Wilkins, my lad, you'll be Sergeant Wilkins yet,
if you play your cards right."

He walked up and he walked down, to make sure; and he decided in his own mind that the stranger was watching Sir Richard's house, though apparently he was idling about to smoke a cigarette in the cool of the evening.

"Now, I wonder whether Sir Richard's in or out?" said P.C. Wilkins; "anyhow, I won't go far away. Who's him? Oh, that thayatrical chap as goes after the nuss."

This remark was made as Abram Higgs slowly slouched up to the area gate, opened it as if he had done so a great many times before, and then slouched down.

"Nice time he has on it!" muttered P.C. Wilkins; "good supper, and as much as he likes to drink. Good ale they have down there, too, I'm told. What's this?"

He took a few rapid strides along the pavement; for, as a carriage approached, he saw the strange Frenchman suddenly start, and come to meet it. But he walked slowly by, as if uninterested on seeing who got out; and then, for the first time noticing the policeman, he carefully drew from one of his side pockets a tiny white poodle pup, with a blue ribbon round its neck, and began to smooth and stroke it, holding it up to some ladies who were passing, as if offering it for sale.

"Won't do, my knowing one," said P.C. Wilkins to himself. "You're a dog fancier, are you; and you want to sell that there dog? But it won't do. It might blind a French policeman, but it won't do, my French cock robin; and I shall put salt on your tail, as sure as a gun! You're about as much like a dog fancier, you are, as I am; and you've got some little game on, that's what you've got, and I'm about the man as'll find you out."

But P.C. Wilkins did not make much progress that day. It was a doctor's carriage that drove up; and after a time he saw the doctor come out and cross the pavement, going as delicately as did King Agag of old. Then the carriage drove off, the Frenchman smoked more cigarettes and fondled his dog, P.C. Wilkins seemed to be busy watching a crossing-sweeper at the corner, carriages passed, footmen came out to cool themselves on the doorsteps of the different houses and ornament the posts, the lamps were lit, the stars looked down on the great square, and nothing happened.

But there was a little more movement inside Sir Richard Lawler's house; for her ladyship had had a desperate quarrel with her lord—so it was said down in the servants' hall. Jane gave her version on the top of James's, contradicting a good deal of what he had said; but announcing that when she took young master into the dining-room at dessert time, her ladyship had got red eyes, and told her to take the child away. Then the little fellow had wanted to go to his papa, and get some fruit; but he had ordered her off.

"In the vishusest way as never was," said Jane, smoothing down her apron.

The next minute Jane had, like the rest, been startled by a cry from upstairs, and the news soon spread that her ladyship was in violent hysterics, and that the groom had gone in a cab from the mews behind to fetch Sir Brandon Cure.

Of course this was the signal for a long canvass of the Rivière fracas, which increased not slightly in its incidents under discussion.

The doctor came ; her ladyship was better— she had been heard to say that she would have a divorce ; Sir Richard had called Mr. Sellars the butler a something or another old fool, and the portly old gentleman had nearly fainted. These and many other things had to be considered ; and by eight o'clock it had been decided by the conclave that there would be a divorce ; that the establishment at Grosvenor-square would be broken up, and that the sooner they all began to look out for fresh situations the better.

"All of us except Miss Jane," said James, meaningly.

"And why shouldn't I look out too ?" said the young lady in question.

"Oh, I'm sure I don't know, if you don't."

"Well, I shouldn't," said Jane, sturdily.

"No, of course not," laughed James—"he, he, he!"

"Because," said Jane, not heeding the interruption, "I should keep to my dear child. Come what may, I'd never leave him."

"Oh, no, I dare say not," laughed James. "You're very fond of him, aint you?"

"Yes, I am," said Jane, "bless him! He's a little limb, I know, but that's only his spirit; for a dearer, more affectionate little fellow never lived, and he loves me quite as much as he does his ma."

"That aint why you won't look out, Jane," said James, grinning.

"Then, why is it then, please, Mr. Clever?" said Jane, defiantly.

"Because—because—there, I won't tell you," sneered James; "your face is as red as a turkey-cock's now."

"You may say what you like for me," said

Jane, carelessly. "I'm not going away, so I tell you."

"Not till somebody comes," sneered James; and at that moment the door opened to admit the scullery-maid, who came up to Jane's side to whisper, in a voice heard all over the hall—

"If you please, Jane, here's Mr. Higgs."

CHAPTER XVIII.

FREE.

D O you know Coldbath Fields Prison, one
side of which, with the entrance gate,
abuts on Coldbath-square, a cheerful
locality from whatever way you approach—up-
hill from dingy Gray's Inn-lane, downhill from
Meredith-street, or from the flanks? There
used to be a tree in Coldbath-square, which
seemed as if the cold bath had been too great a
shock to its system, for that tree died after getting to a fair size. But still it stood, and was
useful; for it formed a corner into which area
railings were fitted, and it got to be in time a
trunk of polished wood, not French polished,

but English and Irish—for the shoulders of in-
numerable people were rubbed against it as they
stood out there and waited.

It may not have occurred to everybody, but
there are two or three classes of people who—to
use the slang phrase—"do their bit" in a gaol ;
notably there are the wilfully vicious and the
unfortunate. Now these people, irrespective of
class, have friends ; and, as a rule, the more wilfully vicious a person may be—in plainer
English, the greater scoundrel—the larger his
circle of acquaintances ; while of those who
appertain to the unfortunate the number may be
very small.

As a matter of course, when Bill, or Jack, or
Sally gets into trouble, there is a large assembly
of friends to see him or her in the court, and
give a cheer when he or she goes off to the van ;
but notably is that assemblage increased when,
the month or the six weeks being ended, the
said Bill, Jack, or Sally is to come out of gaol
—the friends assembling at an early hour out-

side the prison gates, and waiting to give their comrade an ovation.

You may see them on certain mornings outside any of the great prison gates, and notably lounging about Coldbath-square, the dingy walls of which delectable spot give them leaning room for hours and hours. There are some strange types here. The truly unfortunate—a wretched, hollow-eyed woman, in clean rags, waiting to be the first to welcome a husband; a tottering old man, staring dull-eyed at the gate which shall open by and by for the exit of a daughter; a stricken mother on the watch for the son who fell away that once, she is sure, from temptation stronger than he could resist; and in spite of a feeling of loathing she stands right in the thick of the little crowd, that she may be the first to see him, lest evil companions shall be in waiting, and counteract the good that she would do.

She is very neatly dressed, this woman, and her eyes are red yet with the tears she could

not keep down before she came; and it is hard
upon her to listen to the two red-armed, slat-
ternly wenches who are waiting for Tom, who
said he could "do his bit upon his head," having
received two months for some innocently playful
robbery with violence, a repetition of which will
ensure him the cat, and years in place of
months.

They were all there, these same types of people, one dingy, wet morning, when the fog and
blacks hung heavy in the air; and they were sup-
plemented, too, by a few noisy Irish of both
sexes from Gray's Inn-lane, waiting for a couple
of "boys," who had been too liberal with the
stick and their boots in a row.

"Why don't they let 'em out?" said one.

"An' its jist wanting me behind them they
are, the dirty omadhauns!" exclaimed another,
in a high-pitched Milesian tenor.

But the gate did not open, and the watchers
stayed on, comparing notes on crime and
punishment that made more than one shiver.

"Ah," said one woman, with a sigh, "it's all very well to talk about not being long, and not being long; but it takes a great piece out of a man's life every time he's locked up, and he's got nothing to show for it at all."

She was quite right; for of all the ways of living fast, perhaps imprisonment is the most killing. Condemn a well-educated man of thirty to fifteen or twenty years' penal servitude, and ask a statistician what are his chances of living to the end of his time. Very few, you will find. While in a state of freedom, he might have reached to sixty, seventy, or eighty. It is living fast to be dissipated; but a prisoner runs, unknown to himself, very rapidly through his span of life. To him the days seem to crawl, and he gets confused at last, even to mingling one with the other; but life is winging away at an express rate. The candle is for him burning rapidly at both ends.

That month's imprisonment sapped as far into Rivière's constitution as two years of ordinary life. The turnkeys got into the habit of calling him the " French lion," anc ̣ ̣ ʋınt out to this day the cell he occupied, worn by his rapid steps, as he walked ceasel ̣sly up and down whenever he could find himself free from prison routine.

He had had no communication with the outer world, accepting stolidly his fate, and sitting and planning for the future. He did not know then, but the newspaper report never reached Marie. Neither did it come under the notice of Lady Lawler, who only knew of the facts from her husband, who was lamb-like now in his attentions; for her ladyship was confined for a fortnight to her bed, Sir Brandon Cure declaring her situation to be most precarious. There was a breach, though, now between husband and wife, which grew wider every day, though Rivière knew it not.

And now the month was up, and the hour of release came. The gate opened, and, faint and trembling, Rivière hurried out into the presence of the little crowd waiting so anxiously for those they called their own. He could not help shuddering as he heard the various comments and encountered each gaze, wishing the while that it was blackest night, in order that he might escape unnoticed.

It was like running the gauntlet, that first getting away; and even after he had passed into the busy streets, it seemed to him that every one he met stared hard at him, and remarked that he was a felon.

He was partly right, for his appearance did excite attention; people stared very hard at the strange, wild-looking man, whose sunken hollow eyes were full of fire, and glanced angrily right and left, as if in search of an enemy. However, he dived down the most secluded streets, and hurried on towards Soho, his heart beating strangely as he neared the spot where was all he held dear in life.

But now a strange feeling of vacillation came over him, and he dared not enter the street. A cold perspiration stood upon his forehead, and he leaned against a railing for support. Then recovering himself somewhat, he staggered on to one of the cafés which he had been in the habit of frequenting, and taking out the few pence that had been returned to him that morning, he called for and hastily swallowed a petit verre.

This recovered him; and he sat down for a while, looking round carelessly at the occupants of the place, to see face after face without either recognition or retention. He might have noticed that he was an object of remark; but his thoughts were of that room that he was about to visit, and he rose slowly, gave one glance round, and then passed out, trying hard to summon up courage for his task. But, no; something seemed to draw him back—to keep him now that he was free: he seemed to be tenfold a prisoner; and at last he hurried into the square, and began to walk round and round the railings, thinking over the past as well as his confused mind would permit, and calculating the chances of a reconciliation.

Calling himself a coward and a fool, he at length strode boldly down the street, found the door open, and hurriedly ran up the stairs to the second floor, where he paused for a few moments in indecision; then hurriedly turning the handle, he entered, to find himself in a comfortably furnished apartment, face to face with a strange woman and his landlady.

He had come into the wrong room? No there could be no mistake : that was the window where he had sat and seen Lemaire. He knew it by that particular crack, starring one pane ; otherwise, but for the landlady's presence, he might have thought that he was in the wrong house.

For a few seconds there was silence—the women starting back, half frightened.

"Thousand pardons!" said Rivière at last. "But my wife?"

"What, don't you know, sir?" said the landlady, looking pale and agitated, visibly trembling before her lodger.

"I know, woman!—know what?"

"I thought, sir—"

"Well, speak.   Do you not see that I am in agony?   What should I know?"

"I thought you had fetched her—told her to—"

"Will you speak out?" cried Rivière, furiously. "Where is my wife?"

"She's gone, Mister Rivvyer," said the woman, taking refuge in an assumption of anger; "and what's more—"

"Stop!" he exclaimed, waving his hand in a dazed way. "Speak slowly—I am confused. You—say—she is gone," he continued, huskily "Where has she gone?"

"Ah, that's what I want to know," said the landlady, whose voice was now gathering force. "It's hard lines, I can tell you, letting lodgings to such people. But perhaps you have come to—"

"Woman !" said Rivière, huskily, "I want my wife. You say she has gone. She should not have been left, but I was forced away. Now tell me"—he gasped here—"did any one come while I was away? No, no, impossible! She left a note?"

The landlady shook her head.

"Well, a message? Give it me. Do you not see my anxiety?"

"She didn't leave nothing—nothing at all," said the landlady, uneasily. "She went away sudden a fortnit ago, and that's all that I or anybody knows about it. And this lady's been here a week."

"But a moment—listen!" said Rivière. "I am surprised—I do not understand. Did any one come to see her—to take her away?"

"No one but that gentleman as used to meet her in the streets. He came twice that I saw, perhaps more."

"And—and—"

"Did they go away together? Well, I'm not

going to say they did, nor I'm not going to say they didn't. All I know is, that Mrs. Rivvyer went away, and I've never seen her since."

" Mon Dieu!"

CHAPTER XIX.

LOST.

NO words could express the agony of the tone in which Rivière uttered those two words, as the desolate man, hunted ever as it were by fate, gazed wildly for a few moments from one woman to the other; and then, after clutching vainly at one or two pieces of furniture, reeled and fell heavily to the ground.

For a few moments the two women called loudly for help—vainly, though; for at that hour they were the only occupants of the house. Then, recovering themselves, they fetched water, vinegar, salts, and bathed the face of the stricken man till he showed signs of revival.

"There, I don't see why one should make all this fuss over a furriner, who was always a bad lodger," said the landlady. "They owe me over a month now; and his wife going off like that without notice, and leaving me with them bits of things—and not much of them—to keep in the lumber attic till they pay."

"He's getting better now, poor thing," said the other woman. "Poor fellow, how bad he looks! Has she run away from him?" she whispered.

"No—no—no," cried Rivière, starting up—"it is not true—she was too loyal. I will know all about it. I will find her if she's in this world; and, mon Dieu, if she has gone to another, I will follow," he added, softly. "But—I am better now—tell me, she went away? When?"

"A fortnight ago this very day."

"Did she tell no one she was going?"

"No; the gentleman I told you of came two or three times. He said he was a doctor, and knew madame. He wanted to nurse her when the baby was born, but—"

"What?" cried Rivière—"she was ill?"

"Oh, yes, I forgot you did not know. She was took bad the night you left, and did not come back. She wouldn't see that doctor, and I fetched her mine."

Rivière gasped.

"And why did she go? You drove her away. You were harsh to her."

"Which it's jest what I wasn't," said the woman, trembling. "If she'd been my own sister I couldn't ha' done more."

"But why—why, then, did she leave?"

"Perhaps she thought you wouldn't come back to her again, and she took off and went back home."

Rivière thought for a moment, and then shook his head.

"There must have been another reason," he said.

"I don't know what, then," said the landlady;

"only that the French doctor came that morning, for I see him there, talking to her, standing just where you are now, and her standing up before him, with the lovely little baby-girl in her arms."

Rivière started, and shivered with excitement.

"He didn't stop long, and I only saw her twice afterwards; but she was very low, and in the evening, when I went up to ask her if she'd had any news, she was gone, and taken the baby with her, and nothing else, not so much as a band-box."

Rivière, weak with prison fare, reeled once more; but he caught at a chair back, and steadied himself, till the room, which seemed to move round, ceased to revolve before his eyes.

The women tremblingly awaited his recovery, expecting violent manifestations of grief, and a display of excitement similar to the last; but they were deceived, for slowly moving to a chair, he sat for a few moments with his eyes closed, then he looked from one to the other in a strange, half-dazed fashion, as of one who had been stunned.

At last, he rose to go.

"Now, don't take on, that's a good man," said the landlady; "I ain't a-going to say a word about the rent."

"Don't speak to me yet," said Rivière, speaking in a slow, laborious fashion. "I am ill—I am tired."

He walked to the open window, and stood looking out—seeing no one, but being seen; for there had been a watch kept upon him from the prison gates.

The two women stood watching him for a few moments, as he once more made his way to a chair, sat down, and covered his face with his hands, rested his elbows on his knees, and seemed to be trying to collect his thoughts. Then he spoke, in a cold, hard voice—

"Tell me again, I have lost it—tell me all you know."

"But you aint fit to hear it now, my poor dear," said the landlady, kindly.

"Tell me again all you know," said Rivière, sharply; and the woman obeyed, repeating her words, and telling—not all—of her lodger's sudden disappearance.

"You did not see her go — whether any one was with her?" said Rivière, softly; and his voice was so altered that his hearers started.

"No—nothing more than I have told you," said the landlady. "She said once, when she was worried, that you had forsaken her in her trouble for some one else; and begged of me not to turn her away—just, you know, as if I could have been such a beast. But, now, come downstairs to my rooms, and I'll make you a cup of tea directly; and then you can lie down on the sofy for a bit, and you'll be better after. Lord, ma'am," she continued, addressing her tenant, "if there's a blessing in this world in disguise, it's tea, and no end of good it's done me in my time.

But come on down now, Mister Rivvyer, there's a good man."

She approached him, and took his arm as she spoke; but he slowly rose and shook himself free.

"No, no," he said softly, stretching out his hands the while, in a blind, helpless fashion—"she has gone, and I must find her—must find her. She is mine—my wife. Oh, Marie, Marie—and in this strange land!"

There was a wild pathos in the way in which he called for the lost one that thrilled the listeners, and brought tears to their eyes, as they stood watching him till he had descended half the stairs, when the landlady recovered herself.

"He mustn't go like that, poor soul—he'll be jumping off one of the bridges, or poisoning himself at the chemist's! Do you go down and stop him. I can't, for the trembling as there is in my poor legs is something awful."

The lodger hesitated, for she was trembling too. But after a few moments, she went to the

door, hesitated again, and then they both went
down together; but they were too late : Rivière
had left the house—bent, aged, and wan, to
creep slowly over the flags from street to street,
muttering softly—

"I must find her—must find her, even if she
be lost to me for ever."

Then, on and on he went, and ever with a
dark shadow dogging his steps, till the night
fell chill and gloomy—fit time for murder,
should it be abroad.

CHAPTER XX.

BETWEEN LOVERS.

IT was a busy evening in Grosvenor-square,
for Sir Richard and Lady Lawler were
"at home." Carpet had been laid down
over the steps, and awning fitted up by
Aquila. Somebody, florist to the Royal Family,

had sent covered vans and men, who had turned the hall and grand staircase into a conservatory of rich exotics. The confectioner's men, too, had been there busy enough. Cards of invitation had been issued, enough to fill the house again and again, from garret to basement ; and people said it was not before it was time, for the Lawlers had been very quiet of late. Rout seats were placed here and there ; maids stationed behind refreshment tables ; three extra waiters had been sent by the confectioner ; and all bade fair to be a great success.

In the servants' hall, the party had been canvassed with many a nod and wink—Mr. Sellars, whose opinion ruled on account of his grey hairs and position, saying that he might think this way and he might think that way ; perhaps this party was in honour of a making-it-up between Sir Richard and her ladyship, and perhaps it wasn't ; all he'd got to say was, that he was very pleased to find things were going to be as they used to be.

James, footman, on the same afternoon, had taken advantage of Jane, nurse, on her descending to the lower regions, and placing his arm round her waist, again tried to steal a kiss— getting, instead of the kiss, a sounding smack on the ear, which sent forth a cloud of violet powder, and a request to know what he meant by such impudence. Whereat, James, footman, said it was quite correct, for only half an hour before he had seen Sir Richard do so to her ladyship; Jane going off in a huff, with a request that Mr. James would keep his hands to himself for the future, and please recollect that she was engaged.

It was open house in the evening, and Mr. Sellars had himself ordered the big ale jack to be refilled and placed in the servants' hall, intimating that by and by there would be a glass or two of wine, and coffee, and what-not, to be added when the company was on the way. The livery servants fraternized with the waiters, and with the confectioner's men; the maids had on their new caps; and cook was dressed an hour earlier, for she would be at liberty. The two nurses were the only servants who had not much chance of mixing in the rejoicings below stairs; but Jane got over the difficulty by promising to give up her next Monday out to her aide, if she would take full charge of the child, and allow the said Jane to go downstairs.

The fact of it was that upon so joyous an occasion, when choice tit bits ad libitum would be on the way, several servants' friends had received hints to come, and amongst them Abram Higgs; and as the evening progressed there was not much difficulty of access down the area steps to the servants' hall and other parts of the house. The milkman had found that out, and imbibed freely; so had the policeman on duty— though, of course, his visit below was only to see that all was right, and that no improper characters made their way into the house when there was so much plate lying about.

Visitors came, and visitors went; clustered on

the stairs; squeezed into the hot rooms; stood
in doorways; or listened to the singing of
Madame Contraltino and Signor Sottovoce. The
maids behind the tables dispensed refreshments,
and the confectioner's waiters took matters very
easily. Ladies' dresses were pierced by gentlemen's patent leather boots, and crush hats were
waved, tucked under arms, and even sat upon
by their owners. All went on prosperously
above stairs; while below, the servants' friends
picked chicken bones, sipped lukewarm ices, and
partook of the remnants of the lobster salad.

Lady Lawler seemed in the highest spirits,
receiving her guests, and Sir Richard all smiles.

As for Jane, after feasting her eyes by gazing
over the bannisters at the ladies' dresses, she
took one more glance at the sleeping boy; admonished Sarah not to leave him for a moment; and then slipped down the back stairs,
to be soon enjoying a tête-à-téte with Abram
Higgs, to whom she confided the fact that Sir
Richard and her ladyship had "made it up," and

that all the troubles caused by those French people had blown over now for good. Sir Richard had been jealous, and no wonder, seeing how her ladyship had acted; but that was all passed and gone now, and matters were all going smooth.

Here, as there were so many interruptions to the tête-à-tête, and nods, and winks, and remarks from ribald servants and waiters, Jane, seeing that her lover was very properly taking umbrage, and fearful of a disturbance, led him quietly to a back room on the ground floor, a place half study, half museum, where Sir Richard's fishing rods and guns were kept, in company with peculiar hats and garments worn in the chase. The said room had this night been devoted to the reception of odds and ends likely to be in the way of the guests; and being at the end of the passage, and dark, it formed a pleasant substitute for a grove for the lovers, who were soon continuing their tête-à-tête uninterrupted and alone.

Perhaps it was the darkness, and Jane could not see it; but certainly she did not flinch when by some means Abram Higgs' arm crept round her waist; neither did she shrink away when Abram drew her a little closer to him, and meditated a salute.

"And so Sir Richard and her ladyship's quite made it up, have they, eh?" said Higgs.

"Yes, quite now, and I'm glad of it," said Jane; "for the house has been awfully miserable lately."

"Then why don't we make it up more, Jane, dear?"

"I don't know what you mean," said Jane, innocently.

"Why don't we get married?"

"Oh, such nonsense! whoever heard of such a thing?" cried Jane.

"You see, we might be so happy. It would be so nice bringing my wages home every week; while as to now, I often says to myself, ' What's the good of having wages at all?'"

"Ah, there's plenty of time to talk about that yet," said Jane.

"I don't know so much about that," said Mr. Higgs. "All flesh is grass, you know, and some people make hay of it often, long before they expect it."

"What's that?" said Jane, in a sharp whisper, creeping closer to her lover.

"What's what?" said Abram, approving of the movement.

"I thought I heard something," said Jane.

"It was only my 'art beating responsive," said Abram, recalling a little of the last love scene he had witnessed at the Royal Soho Theatre.

"Don't talk stuff," said matter-of-fact Jane.

"'Tisn't stuff, dear," said her lover. "Now, do name the day, and—"

"Oh," whispered Jane, "I know there's some one in here listening. Let's go."

As she spoke, there was a faint rustling noise,

and one of the weapons hung upon the wall
seemed to have been touched.

"Let me have a go-in at him," whispered
Abram, in the same tone. "It's one of them
waiters—I see him watching us before."

"No, no—come away," said Jane, softly; and
taking her swain's hand, she led him softly out
of the room in the dark, closed the door, and
then, watching their opportunity, they once
more reached the servants' hall; but to enjoy
no further intercourse, for there were too many
people about; and soon after, Jane declaring
that she must return upstairs, Abram walked
along the passages with her to the area door,
in no very pleasant state of mind.

"I don't believe there was anybody up in that
room," he said, gruffly.

"Ah, indeed there was," said Jane, trying to
mollify him.

"Only us," he replied; "and you wanted to
get rid of me."

"No, indeed, Abram. I heard some one

moving as plainly as possible, and, of course, I wasn't going to stay to have everything we said listened to. When are you coming again?"

"I don't know," said Abram, gruffly. "I don't see as it's much use my coming—you don't care; and when I do get here, all you think about's how to get me away again."

"It's a shame to talk so. I never treat you like that, dear."

That "dear" had the required effect, and the two parted the best of friends, after another appointment for an afternoon soon, Mr. Higgs announcing that it would be long before his duties would allow of another evening visit.

CHAPTER XXI.

AN UNINVITED GUEST.

TWO hours had passed, and the last visitor departed. The confectioner's men had hastily collected together the relics of the refreshments; and along with soaked wafers, melted ices, and heeltaps of negus and sticky jellies, the flowers and ornaments turned sickly and faded in the heat. Mr. Sellars had seen to his chamber candlesticks, and gone to bed; the maids had all, save her ladyship's, retired; the two livery servants had been asleep some time—one in a chair with his head in a corner, the other with his head stuck fast to the hall table.

Jane had reached the nursery region, to find the little boy awakened by the music, and now perfectly disinclined for sleep; the result being that his nurse had to amuse him as best she could, till the little thing condescended to drop off to sleep once again. And now, at last thoroughly weary, Jane stood thinking of bed, and also about the pressing invitations of Abram Higgs to marry. She stepped to the door, and opened it, to listen whether all below had gone to rest. All was quite dark and still, and she was about to close the nursery door and retire to rest, when she heard a door downstairs open and shut suddenly, and directly after a thrill of terror ran through her as she heard a faint scream.

For a few moments the girl stood irresolute ; then, nerving herself with the idea that her mistress was ill, she ran across the landing to her ladyship's bed - room, and roused the maid, who was nodding in an easy chair.

"Here, Mrs. Henning—quick!" she cried, "her ladyship's ill."

"Where?" exclaimed the startled maid.

"In the lib'ry, I think," cried Jane; and, with beating heart, she ran hurriedly downstairs followed more slowly by the maid, who stopped short when she reached the first landing, and clung to the balustrade, afraid to descend farther.

Upon reaching the hall, voices could be heard, and the half-open library door showed Jane that she was right in her surmises.

Without pausing, she ran in, and then stopped, startled by the sight that met her gaze.

In front of her, supporting Lady Lawler, who had fainted, was her master, glancing fiercely at the squalid - looking form of the Frenchman, who, with raised and denunciatory hand, and his back to Jane, was speaking in a low, hissing whisper—

"It is as well, perhaps, that she cannot hear. Poor thing, I have no ill-feeling towards her;

but as to you, you have earned my bitterest
hate. I do not strike you now, because, with
your coward hand, you would ring for the servants and the police. You would send me
again to prison—the strong, victorious over
the weak. I cannot spare myself for prison,
now—I have a task to perform. I came to-
night, though, as I have said, determined to
see you; and I am here to tell you that you
have robbed me of all I loved. You have
struck at me through the heart. So now, mind
this : I have been innocent of all crime towards
you. Your jealousy of that poor thing has
been madness — suspicion of one pure as a
child. But I will have revenge upon you. As
you have struck at me through my tenderest
feelings—as through you I have lost all I
loved, so I will strike at you when you least
expect. Sir Richard Lawler, *au revoir !*"

"No, no !—no, no !" shrieked Lady Lawler,
who had heard the latter part of his speech, and
who now strove to escape from her husband's

arm, and throw herself at their unwelcome visitor's feet. "No, no! I have been to blame for this, Monsieur Rivière."

"No, no! It is I, and I have said," he replied, turning coldly away, and before Sir Richard could well recover from his surprise the door had closed, and Lady Lawler was sobbing hysterically upon the breast of Jane.

"At last," cried Sir Richard, as one of the servants, sleepy and half stupefied, appeared at the door through which Rivière had passed a few moments before. "I have rung four times. Stop that man—fetch the police."

"What man, Sir Richard?" stammered the servant; and as he spoke the dull reverberation of the front door told that action was too late.

Resigning his wife to the maid, however, Sir Richard rushed out into the hall, tore open the door, and then dashed hatless into the square, to gaze up and down, to see nothing but the twinkling lamps; and feeling that any attempt at pursuit would be worse than folly, he returned to the library, to find that Lady Lawler was recovering, and hysterically explaining to the maid how that, just as they were about to retire, the door had opened, and Monsieur Rivière had appeared.

"His face was horrible, Jane," sobbed her ladyship. "Did you see it?"

"No, m' lady, his back was to me," said Jane; "but please don't take on."

"No, Jane, no—I'm better now; but how could he have got in?"

Jane thought of the noise she had heard in Sir Richard's room that evening; but she kept her own counsel. It was plain that any one who knew the house might have made a way in that night, and the scene was now ended by the entrance of Sir Richard, who bade the nurse help her mistress up to her bed-room, where he did not follow for some hours, but sat moodily in his study, wondering whether Rivière's were but empty threats, or whether he should have to be prepared some day to battle with the Frenchman's revenge.

"Pooh!" ejaculated the baronet, at last. "What folly! The poor wretch can only have been out of prison for a few hours, and he is bitter and spiteful. That is all."

He went up to bed; but he could not make his mind so easy. Strange dreams assailed him, and undefined terrors of the future; and at last he woke, trembling and beaded with sweat, to lie, thoughtful and anxious, wondering, in spite of himself, what form the Frenchman's revenge would take, and whether he ought in some way to be prepared. Should he once more set the law in force?

The answer came—No! The threats were not worthy of his notice.

CHAPTER XXII.

AGAIN.

SIR RICHARD LAWLER, when he ran out of his house, had not looked in the right direction, or he would have seen that Rivière, after stepping quickly down the steps, had not gone far before, anticipating pursuit, he had turned into the shadow of a dark doorway, where he stood smiling bitterly as he saw Sir Richard come blundering out and run hurriedly past him, to stand staring up and down.

"Poor fool!" he muttered, as he saw the baronet turn back. "Bah! but he has no brains. He is a great boy."

Then he waited a few minutes, heard the door bang as Sir Richard re-entered, and merely stopping to roll up a cigarette, he stepped quietly out into the square once more, and sauntered thoughtfully along.

He seemed very calm and impassive now, and went straight on in an aimless fashion, apparently seeing nothing, till he encountered some wretched woman or another loitering about the corner of some street—a poor miserable, who, from being as dull and apathetic as himself, would on his approach commence humming softly the fag-end of some popular ditty, as if her heart were so over-flowing with gladness that this was the safety valve for getting rid of so much joy. Then, beneath some lamp-post, haggard eyes would gaze into eyes made more haggard with paint, and Rivière would pass on, shaking his head.

For quite two hours he sauntered thus about the West-end, never seeming to tire, and ever keeping to the main, well-lit streets. Cabs and

late carriages passed him; and then the echoes
of the streets would only be broken by the
noisy, jolting rumble of some heavy-laden
wagon, coming in from the country with its
freshly cut vegetables for the morning's market,
horses and driver looking of a sleepy sameness
in the dim light.

Once or twice he sat down on a step to rest,
and lean his head upon his hand, evidently
thinking deeply; but always, as if by instinct,
choosing a step that was close to and well-lit by
a lamp. Then, before arising, he would glance
up and down the street in an uneasy way, as if
he expected to see some one following him; but,
as a rule, all was silent and deserted.

Rested somewhat, he would rise and go
slowly on in the same restless manner, to pause
now and then, and look up at a window where a
light illumined the drawn blind, and flickering
shadows told of sickness within, even as did the
hurried messenger he saw in one street, who
sharply crossed the road as if pursuing him, and

made Rivière turn like a wild animal at bay.
But the man passed on, and he saw him run
down the next street, where a red, glowing eye
shone out of the darkness, like a danger signal
on the railroad of life, telling where lived the
pointsman who might have it in his power to
shunt the traveller on to the safe main line, or
into that narrow siding whose end is death.

Rivière's heart beat more rapidly for a few
moments till he saw where the messenger was
bound. This sent his thoughts back to the
room at Soho, where he painted in imagination
the scene at Marie's sick couch, the attendant
doctor, and Lemaire's importunities, till his
fists involuntarily clenched, and he stood, with
rugged brow, glaring before him into the night.

As the time passed, he grew more and more
thoughtful, and his pace more slow. At times
he quite halted, and more than one policeman
turned to look upon him—P.C. some number or
another, in his zeal, turning the shade of his
bull's-eye so that the light flashed for a moment

on the sallow, troubled face; but, as the stranger was moving on, he did no more.

It was singular, though, that on two occasions Rivière had no sooner turned a corner than a dark, lithe figure seemed to spring up, from no one could tell where, dart to the corner, and remain watching till the soft, slow footsteps died away.

This occurred again and again; but Rivière passed on through street after street, growing less cautious as he became more weary, choosing now, or involuntarily taking, the side streets in his devious way.

He had gone on like this for quite three hours, incessantly smoking cigarette after cigarette, which he rolled up occasionally upon the doorsteps where he sat to rest; but at last nature showed symptoms of giving up, his pace became slower, and his pauses upon doorsteps more frequent, and each time of longer duration.

At last, in a dreary street off Tottenham-court-road, he sat down, after turning a corner, and tearing a leaf of paper from a little book, he slowly rolled up another cigarette. He had to collect the very dust out of his box to get a sufficiency of tobacco for this last one; and he sighed as he moistened the paper to make it adhere, for he knew that two or three hours must elapse before he could get a fresh supply of that which was to him now a solace in his miserable tramp.

"My faith!" he ejaculated, as he rose and took out another box to get a fusee; "but it is too bad—the last light has gone!"

What should he do? Climb to one of the lamps, and get a light? No, he could not do that—some one might pass with a lighted pipe. He had only to wait. But where was he?

He looked about, but did not recognize his whereabouts: one street, if dark and dingy, was so much like another; and he shook his head and walked on—stopped—thought. Why should he go any farther in this aimless way? He could not sit down and sleep—it was too wet and cold. No ; here was an object. He would see if he could retrace his steps, street by street, to Grosvenor-square, where he could stand and think ; and by that time it would be daylight, the sun would rise warm and bright, and the park was near, where he could go and seek out a retired spot, and sleep restfully upon the soft grass, and forget everything for a while.

It was very dark now, and very cold. The street was gloomy and silent; and, as he turned to go back, he shivered again and again with cold, and an instinctive nervous apprehension, which made him gaze anxiously up and down the street, and peer into the different doorways he passed.

If he had but had a light ! It was so provoking, when he held that little cigar between his teeth. But it was hard—very hard—this life. Why had he not been left in peace in his own home ? But what was this ?

He had just turned the corner, on his way back into a street more gloomy and silent than that which he had left, and as he turned it was to become aware of a dark figure crouching in the doorway of a house—knees drawn up, arms clutching them, and head resting on its breast. It was all plainly to be seen, for there was a lamp on the opposite side, which shot a few rays right into the doorway.

Rivière paused for a few moments, with all the suspicion of a hunted man ; then he was about to pass hurriedly away, but he saw something, half hidden by the figure's position, which made him stay. It was evidently a street-seller of matches, and that was his box, hugged up to his chest.

" He would give me one," thought Rivière. " I cannot buy ; but the poor are generous to the poor. It is cruel to wake him ; but he will forgive me."

He stepped to the doorway, and bending down, touched the crouching figure, which seemed thin and slight as that of a boy ; but a heavy, stertorous breath was the only response.

"Will you give me one match ?" said Rivière, in a low voice—"just one. I am like you, out in the streets for the night."

What followed was like magic ; but quick as was the action, far quicker was thought, and with a flash Rivière knew that with all his caution he had deliberately stepped into a trap ; for as he bent down, at one and the same moment a thin, nervous hand caught him by the throat, he became aware of a light step behind, and by the ray of the distant lamp he saw the flashing gleam of a small, keen blade, as it darted up, poising for a deadly blow.

CHAPTER XXIII.

THE GLOSSY STRANGER.

A!" said Mr. Sellars, the butler, taking off his spectacles, and laying down the *Times*, which he always made a point of going over very carefully before he let Sir Richard or his lady have a glance. Nominally, the purpose for which Mr. Sellars took the paper was to air it—to change it from a damp, limp sheet, to one that was crisp and rattled as it was moved; but this airing took a long time, for Mr. Sellars always read the police reports from beginning to end, and all the short bottom paragraphs that seemed to promise juicily, occasionally favouring the housekeeper or one of the men with an extract read aloud— very kind, no doubt, and well intentioned, but extremely painful to the listener, inasmuch as Mr. Sellars had a habit of bending his neck and letting his chin repose on his breast, while he seemed to direct the whole of his discourse to the central button on his shirt front—his audience often listening in vain.

"Ha!" he said one morning, as he refolded the paper, "my opinion of them French is that they always wants to have some one standing over 'em with a big stick to keep 'em in order, for they're always in hot water over there. What do they want, too, letting loose their roughs to come over here? We've had enough of it with that little Frenchman—a beggar; and what does he do but act like his seck, tell every one he knows how he has got on, and of course they beset the house. Five furreners have we had here in two days with something to sell, and take 'No!' for an answer they won't."

Here a double knock at the front door interrupted his musings, and he stood and listened. Nobody seemed going to answer it, so he went to the housekeeper's room door and shouted "Ennery!"

"Yezzer," came from a distance.

"Front door!"

"I'm cleaning the plate!" cried the same voice, supplementing the remark with a muttered grumble.

"Where's James?"

"Doing the drawn'-room lookin'-glasses," was the reply, followed directly after by a repetition of the knock.

There was no help for it, so Mr. Sellars puffed up the stone staircase and along the hall, where he paused for a moment to lay down his newspaper before going to the door, which he threw open to find upon the step a very dark, black-bearded man, with piercing eyes, jetty brows, no hair to speak of, but what there was spiky and black, peeping out at the sides from beneath the brim of the curliest, glossiest, shortest-napped hat that was ever ironed up to a dazzling polish.

The effect of the glossy hat was, however, to some extent neutralized by the visitor's boots, which were of wonderful crinkly patent leather, very round at the toe, very thin in the sole, and half covered by glossy black trousers, continued under the boots in cloth straps, which held the said pantaloons tight down, as the braces of their owner held them tight up, and made them sit in a series of straight folds from top to sole. His coat, also of glossy black, was pinched in at the waist, and fitted him to perfection, being buttoned over a white vest, beyond which was a black satin something which hid the wearer's shirt front; but his collar and cuffs were prodigious in their size and whiteness, as they appeared above and below that coat. It was a strange coat, too, looking like one of the progeny of a male dress coat and a female frock ditto—

as the tailors say; while to complete the picture, jauntily tied by great silken cords, a flowing cloak, glossy as the rest, hung from the visitor's shoulders.

As Mr. Sellars stood, with puffed-out cheeks, seeing all this, as he glanced at the new arrival from top to toe and back again, he became also aware that the stranger held in one delicately gloved hand a jetty black tasselled walking stick, in the other a card case, from which he was drawing a delicate-looking card.

"Take—thees—to—your—masster," said the visitor, holding out the card, and speaking very deliberately, as if to avoid mistakes of pronunciation.

Mr. Sellars took the card, and looked at it. Then he looked again at the visitor. He was another "furrener," as Mr. Sellars would have called him; but that hat, those boots, that cloak, and, above all, those gloves!

Mr. Sellars was impressed; and though he hesitated, it was with a bad grace. If the

stranger had asked if Sir Richard were at home
at such an out-of-the-way time in the morning,
of course he would have said "No;" but when
such an archangel of fashion and deportment
stood before him, and in the most nonchalant
manner held out a delicate card, and said
"Take this to your master," what was he to
do?

But the visitor was, after all, only a Frenchman; and Mr. Sellars hesitated, glanced at the
card, looked back at the giver, and then shrank
—shrank involuntarily; for the stranger was
fixing him with a pair of eyes that looked out
now from a narrow black slit, so it seemed to
the butler, and for a few moments he stood
helpless and unnerved, till the stranger smiled
blandly, waved one hand, bowed, and Mr.
Sellars backed slowly into the hall, leaving the
visitor upon the doorstep.

Mr. Sellars felt better as soon as he was out
of the range of those eyes. He did not know it
himself, but they had had some influence upon

him sufficient to make him take the card and walk towards the library.

But before he reached the door he paused. Sir Richard had told him he could see no foreigners—no one at all likely to have come from Rivière; and perhaps this might be one of his friends.

He recovered himself, and walked back to the door, only to feel convinced, as he drew near once more, that it was impossible that this glossy stranger could be one of that set.

"If you please, sir," he began, "Sir Richard—"

"Take—thees—to—your—masster," said the stranger, pointing now to the card with his glossy cane.

Mr. Sellars looked in the narrow eyes again, and he was subdued. There was no resisting them. They had a strange effect—such a one as sent him slowly back to the library, telling himself that he must risk it anyhow, even if Sir Richard were cross.

He entered the room with fear and trembling.

Sir Richard was not there.

This was a check. He must be in the drawing-room, so he went up there; but it was only to find James ostensibly polishing the long mirrors, but really grinning at himself and admiring his figure as he stood posed upon a pair of steps.

"Sir Richard aint been here," said that worthy, beginning to polish vigorously, and turning red in the face.

So Mr. Sellars went out softly, crossed the landing, and tapped at the door of her ladyship's boudoir, answered to the "Come in!" and learned that Sir Richard had gone up to his dressing-room.

By this time Mr. Sellars was beginning to pant, for he had a good deal of flesh to carry. There was nothing for it, though, but to proceed; so he panted up to the said dressing-room, to find Sir Richard studiously contemplating a pair of leathers, evidently with ideas of the future hunting season.

"Well?" came the gruff salute.

"A foreign gentleman, sir."

"What?" thundered Sir Richard, in tones that made the butler shrink back, holding the card at arm's length.

"The card, sir—quite the gentleman," stammered the butler.

Sir Richard glanced at the card, without taking it in his hand.

"Some confounded friend," he muttered, gloomily. "No, hang me if I go out!" he exclaimed. "I can't stand a meeting with him. Here, you sir—take the card back, and tell the fellow I won't see him, and if he comes again he will be given into custody. Do it too!" he exclaimed, growing louder and more excited, as he backed Sellars to the door, through which that gentleman gladly escaped, taking even pleasure in the bang which followed his exit, for he feared his angry lord—wrath having the effect upon him of making his stout person feel like so much jelly; consequently, he descended the stairs more hastily than was his wont, growing vexed himself with the visitor who had got him such a snubbing, and ready to pour upon him the vials of his own wrath.

"A-coming here and ordering me about," grumbled Mr. Sellars. "Let him take his dirty bit of pasteboard to some one else. Give him into custody, eh? Yes, I will, and no mistake, if he sauces me; and—eh? what?"

Mr. Sellars stood aghast; for he had reached the front door, card in hand, to find that the stranger had gone.

He stepped out and down the step, looking up and down the square, but there was no one visible: so Mr. Sellars stepped back into the hall, and closed the door, looking very serious as he laid the card down upon the table, puffed his cheeks a little, and then stood upon a mat thinking.

The upshot of his thoughts was that he went to a stand and counted the umbrellas.

All right.

The coats.

None missing.

The hats.

Pooh! he was too well dressed for that. What did he want, then? for it was evident that he had stolen nothing from the hall.

There was some plate, though, in the dining-room—was he after that?

Mr. Sellars broke out in a cold perspiration as he hastened into the big room, and counted the articles upon the sideboard, to find that they were all there; and a visit to the library showed that the big silver inkstand was also safe.

"What's it mean?" said Mr. Sellars, as he stood musing upon the mat; but he could make nothing more of it, only that the stranger was gone, and the card, when read, "Monsieur Alexis Aimée," gave no explanation.

"Depend upon it," said Mr. Sellars, sagely, as he descended to the lower regions, "he got

tired of waiting, and he means to call again.
Ha!" he said, as he got to the housekeeper's
room, and sank with a sigh into his chair; "but
he doesn't know about the police."

CHAPTER XXIV.

"I CARRY A STING."

LOUIS RIVIERE had seen too much danger in his eventful life to be appalled by his position, one which seemed more to appertain to the gloomy piazzas of Venice than to a police-guarded London street; but the stranger, when he comes to our shores, brings with him strange ways, even as the British sailor meets assault in a foreign land with a knock-down blow of his fist.

It was a peculiar position for Rivière, but he had lived so long in peril that an instant sufficed to set aside surprise and place him well upon the alert. Lithe as an eel, as the blow fell he wrenched himself aside ; and before the hand was half raised for a second stroke, Rivière caught his assailant's wrist, holding the stiletto at arm's length, while his own right hand held something pointed and sharp, which glittered in the light.

"I carry a sting, my friend," he hissed as his own wrist was caught in turn, and the two men stood face to face, with burning eyes and throbbing pulses, each knowing that a moment's weakness might mean death.

"You were cunning, my friend," snarled Rivière again, speaking through his teeth, as the almost motionless struggle went on—an awful struggle, from the strange, cold silence of the men. There was no violent writhing or contortion, only hand clasping wrist—each man exerting all his strength in a quiet, nervous pressure, the result for the weaker being that a sharp blade would pierce him as his muscles relaxed.

"Traitor! spy!" hissed his assailant, in reply, as he now made a strong effort, but only to lose ground, for Rivière seemed, like a clever fencer, to meet assault by presenting his point; and at the end of a minute his assailant knew that his chance of fulfilling his mission was gone, bending now his attention to the easiest way of making his escape.

But this was no light matter; for his attack had roused the thirst for blood in Rivière, whose eyes glittered now dangerously, as he pressed his enemy back step by step, step by step, across the pavement and into the road.

Here for a few moments they stood panting, hand still grasping wrist; and yet there was no wild, excited struggle—all took place so silently that not a sound disturbed the quiet of the street.

"Life for life," thought Rivière. "He would have slain me in his treacherous attack, and now—Ah!"

Opportunity seemed to serve him; for his enemy slowly yielded inch by inch, being borne down by Rivière's superior power, till he appeared, as it were, to collapse suddenly, and fall upon one knee. But as Rivière half lost his balance by this sudden giving way, he woke to the fact that it was but a ruse; for his assailant shot up once more, striking the other full in the chest, and driving him backwards. Then, making a rapid blow with his freed hand, the man darted away; and Rivière stood shivering with excitement and listening to the pat, pat, pat of retiring footsteps, as he stood feeling his shoulder and drawing from the thick collar of his coat a tiny, keen little knife, which had missed injuring him by the eighth of an inch.

"Let him go," he muttered; "but, mon Dieu! what would they—am I to be hunted to death?"

The regular pace of a coming policeman aroused him; and for a moment he thought of asking his help, and telling of what had taken place.

"But what good?" he muttered. "I have escaped. I must be my own police for the future, and take care. But it was an escape!"

He went away, shivering nervously, and hardly able to realize the fact that he was uninjured; while as he went along the streets he kept fancying he saw dark figures crouching in every doorway, till he regained the better lighted thoroughfares, where he walked up and down, or rested in the neigbourhood of some cabstand, where there were people about, till broad daylight.

For the space of about a week after this night's work, Rivière, in a desultory way, pursued what he thought was a search for his lost wife. He asked at the different steamboat offices, and made inquiries at the principal termini of the railways — of course, without result; and then, brooding over his loss, he grew more and more imbued with the idea that, believing he had forsaken her, Marie had listened to the persuasions of Lemaire, who had visited her, and then, as soon as she felt strong enough, fled with him to France.

Then he sank into a dull, low, listless state, living he knew not how, but daily sinking mentally and bodily, till he grew more weak and helpless. He went again and again to the Soho lodgings, asking the first time for news; afterwards directing a mute look of entreaty at his old landlady, who often confided to her lodger the fact that "her heart bled for the poor dear man, whose sufferings was terrible to behold." And it was to her kindness that he owed many a night's lodging and many a meal; for he seemed nerveless now, and without the spirit to strike out against the stream that was bearing him away.

He had given over to this woman the little furniture that belonged to him, sufficient in its value to free him from the arrears he owed her; and nothing could have been more honourable than his behaviour, she told him, when one morning he came to bid her farewell.

"And sha'n't I see you no more, Muster Rivvyer?" she said.

"No," he replied, sadly, "no more; but if you should have any news for me, send it by letter to the Poste Restante, and I shall get it—if I am alive," he added, after a slight pause.

The landlady caught him by his thin arm, and gazed anxiously into his wild eyes.

"You're not thinking of any wickedness of that sort, Mr. Rivvyer, are you?" she said, hoarsely. "Don't, don't—please, don't give your mind to that wickedness."

"To what wickedness?" he said, gazing at her vacantly.

"Why—why—you were thinking of going out of the—there, was there ever such a fool as I am, to go and put such an idea into the poor man's head?"

"And why not?" he said, wearily—"why not

go out of the world? I know that was what
you meant. Why not leave here? There is
not room for me in this place—why should I
live?"

"Because—because," exclaimed the woman,
excitedly—"what, what shall I tell him? Oh,
why is not some one here to stop him?" she
muttered to herself. "Because—there, I have
it, thank God for the thought!—because she
might come back."

"Ah!" he exclaimed, almost in a shriek, and
then subsiding into a quiet tone. "Yes, you
have reason—you are right. She might come
back. Yes," he muttered to himself, "she might
come to see whether I was so great a villain
as she believed me. You have reason," he
added, aloud. "Do not tremble for me. I
go; and if you have news for me, you can
write."

Before she could stretch out her hand to stay
him, he had gone; and she stood shaking her
head, thinking of his great troubles, and won-

dering whether he really had so sinister an intention as she surmised, and whether her words had had the effect of turning him into a better frame of mind.

CHAPTER XXV.

A QUIET AFTERNOON.

OR the first few days Sir Richard Lawler troubled himself hugely about the threats of Rivière; but his was not a nature for such utterances to make a deep and lasting impression. At the end of the week the remembrance was growing weaker, and when a fortnight had elapsed he would have ceased to think of it at all, had not Lady Lawler's occasional hysterical fits brought the circumstances back to mind. For the adventure had made a deep impression upon her, sending her into a state of nervous depression, wherein she was constantly imagining that some terrible misfor-

tune was about to fall upon them, in spite of
Sir Richard's smiles at her fears. She joined
with him now, readily enough, in denouncing
Rivière's behaviour, and with tears, asked pardon again and again for her frivolous conduct.
But this was not needed : any division between
man and wife that had previously existed being
now thoroughly healed.

A month passed, and as nothing further had
been seen or heard of Rivière, his threats had
nearly passed from their mind, and Sir Richard
proposed a couple of months in Devonshire to
complete his wife's cure.

The matter was pretty well discussed in the
servants' hall and housekeeper's room, Mr. Sellars announcing his great dislike, from principle,
to the country. The footmen disapproved, too,
of the movement ; and amongst the female
servants, Jane looked rather gloomy at the
prospect of being separated from Mr. Abram
Higgs for a couple of months. She even
debated within herself whether it would not be

sensible on her part to say "Yes" the next time
he asked her a certain question; for what might
not occur during a two months' absence? He
might resent her coldness and forget her, and
that would be terrible; not that she would have
owned to her disappointment, but have bridled
up and said it was a "good job." Anyhow, she
was a great deal more tender to Abram Higgs
the next time he came, imparting so much pleasure to that worthy, that upon parting he
intimated his intention of "running up for an
hour the next afternoon."

The next afternoon arrived, and, fortunately
for the lovers, Sir Richard and Lady Lawler
had gone out, leaving Jane at liberty, since she
thought that her second in command could take
care of little Clive, while she had a pleasant
interview with Abram.

Fortune does not always favour us. Sarah
the under-nurse, was seized with a terrible
bilious headache, and went to bed, leaving the
little boy to Jane, who, to make the best of

things, took him down into the dining-room, ostensibly to see "the gee-gees," but really to enable sapient Jane to watch from the dining-room window for the coming of Mr. Higgs.

Mr. Sellars was taking a nap; the footman was out with the carriage; the under-butler, having laid the cloth, was spelling over the *Times*, which his chief had just let fall; the cook and her underlings were busy enough in the kitchen; housemaid, too, and lady's-maid had gone up—to use their own expressive term —to clean themselves; and all was very quiet and peaceful in the great house. As for the little boy, he toddled about over the Turkey carpet, and hid himself beneath the great table, laughing merrily as he peeped forth from the long damask folds at his nurse, who busied herself in watching from the window, troubling herself very little about the child, as he was so good.

It was a fine bright afternoon, and Jane felt

in excellent spirits. She was not so very angry
with the policeman who went by and nodded
laughingly at her. She recognized, too, the
milkman, when he came and gave her a smile at
the open window where she stood, before he
dragged at the bell, and yelled out his customary falsetto yodel. She looked down
musingly into the area as he rattled his can,
and delivered his milk, tramped up the stone
stairs, and walked off to yell at another area
gate.

Then, as she stood there, a very glossy-
looking, dark, foreign gentleman sauntered
by, stopping by the railings to strike a light
and illumine the cigar he so leisurely took from
a showy case. This gentleman came back,
too, twice ; and made Jane blush by the way
he stared.

But at last he disappeared, to be succeeded
by a shabby-looking man, who came to the
area gate, opened it as if he knew how, and
held up something in a box for sale. Then

an organ grinder came and persistently ground, till the little man with something to sell came again, and pestered the girl to buy, or to exchange some old things for a pair of vases.

" They will do for you when you are married," he said to her; but, although bent in mind upon that pleasant ceremony, Jane would not listen to the voice of the charmer; but watched on till her heart gave a bump, as she caught sight of Abram Higgs coming along by the square railings, and after letting him see her at the window, she turned to the child.

" Now, Clivey will be a good little boy while nurse goes downstairs, won't he?"

The child looked up and laughed, and then resumed his former task of sticking the prongs of a silver fork, which he had drawn from the table, in amongst the long pile of the thick carpet.

The next minute Jane had hurried out of the room, and closed the dining-room door after her, and was running to the head of the stairs, when she encountered housemaid No. 2.

"Oh, Fanny! I'm just going downstairs for a few minutes. I've left Clive in the dining-room; go and have a look at him."

"Yes, as soon as I've been upstairs," was the reply. "I won't be long."

Away went Fanny to her ladyship's room, and away went Jane downstairs into the area; the former to forget the child in the contemplation of two or three new dresses fresh home from the modiste, and laid out on her lady-ship's bed — the latter to forget the child in the sweet discourse of her beloved, for as she went she heard the clang of the area gate.

Half an hour had glided away like thirty seconds, when Fanny turned with a sigh from the dresses, wishing that she had been a lady, and thinking of how she would, had such been the case, have decked her charms. Then she took up her water-can with a sigh, and slowly proceeded downstairs, recollected the little boy when half-way, and hastened to the dining-room to find the table cloth a little dragged at one end, a fork and a couple of table spoons on the carpet; but—no child.

She left the room, and then ran back, thinking that perhaps he was asleep beneath the table. At the same time she saw, too, that the window was partly open, and a chair beneath.

"She's been and fetched him," muttered Fanny; and going back, she took her can, and proceeded to the lower regions, humming a tune as she went along the passage.

Fanny halted as she heard the closing of the area door, and then walked towards her who had shut it; and directly after she stood face to face with Jane.

"Well, said the latter, "where is the child?"

"The child!" exclaimed Fanny, taken aback —"the child!"

"Yes," exclaimed Jane, in a strange tone of voice—"the child. Didn't I ask you to go in to him?—and you haven't been."

"I went just now," said Fanny, snatching at a chance for exculpation.

"Just now!" cried Jane, repeating her words. "I asked you go ever so long ago. I only wanted to come downstairs a minute. But where is the boy?"

"Where is the boy?" stammered Fanny. "I thought you had him."

"I have him!" shrieked Jane. "No, no! I haven't got him. Oh, Fanny, if you've lost him, I'll never forgive you."

"How can I have lost him?" exclaimed Fanny, spitefully. "He must have gone up into the nursery, then, if he isn't down here."

Jane flew by her into the dining-room, ran round it hastily, peered beneath the cloth, and then ran up to the nursery; searched everywhere she could think of; and then came tearing down the stairs, shrieking with all her might—

"The child!—the child!—where is Master Clive?"

END OF VOL. II.

www.ingramcontent.com/pod-product-compliance
Lightning Source LLC
Chambersburg PA
CBHW030759020726
47499CB00006B/1692